Fireside

Christmas

Collection

Volume I

Laura Wiggin

Inspirational

Inklings

www.inspirationalinklings.com

Inspirations

Each story has very real people
or circumstances of which I have drawn
characters from and nestled them into
a Thomas Kincaid picture
depicting Christmas Miracles.

I dedicate this book to those folks dear
to my heart that have inspired
these writings.

Most of all to the One who gives
Christmas it's True meaning
Jesus the Christ

Laura Wiggin has lived a lifetime of writing instead of writing for a lifetime. When the Lord gave her the "pen", He had equipped her with a multitude of life lessons. As a young child she knew quickly the reality of rejection and abuse. But God sent a church bus to rescue her and give her the ride of her life. She got saved at the age of 13. She is happily still married to the man who swept her off her feet at the young age of 17 and has 3 amazing adult sons.

She has walked the pathway of infertility and miscarriages. She had a son with cancer at age 2. As a military wife for 20 years she has moved all over the United States. Two sons joined the military and what they went through no momma should ever know. Woven in through all these years are people God has used in her life.

Her Writing Motto:
If you are not involved with people, you have nothing to write about!

Her Life Motto:
Loving God through loving Others!

Now that her husband is retired and they have settled in a small community in Tennessee where they have jumped in. Laura can be found just about anywhere there are people. Loving on them is her favorite thing. Whether lending a listening ear, or drying a tear, she is out there. Her desire is the share the One that gives us Hope, Jesus!

Her love for writing began years ago when she began to make greeting cards out of paper sacks. Then she found stamps...the rest is history. Her favorite thing is making cards and sending them. She also began to write on quilts and anything else she could get her hands on!

The Lord has blessed her with a tender heart and the gift of encouragement. So, whether you are with her or are reading one of her books...you will come away with a smile on your face and an over flowing cup of encouragement!

OTHER TITLES BY

Laura Wiggin

Orphaned at Home - Series

The Bus Ride (book 1)

The Beat of My Heart (book 2)

Love Finds a Home (book 3)

A Season for Everything – Series

A Season of Rebuilding (book 1)

TABLE OF CONTENTS

Christmas Scraps:

Hanging Mistletoe

"Hi mom."

"Hello Trevor, good to hear your voice. How are you? How is school going?"

"It's going." Janet's 24-year-old son told her.

"I'm so proud of you. You served your country in the military. Now you're going to college, albeit, a few years behind your peers, but you are doing it. Not to mention you are halfway across the United States from your family."

"Thanks, mom, I always love to hear your voice of encouragement. You have always been my loudest cheering section."

"I believe in you, son. You can do anything you set your mind to do." She hated they were miles apart, but he seemed happy. Most importantly, he was following God, and God was doing a work in him, but she did long to see his face.

"How are you and dad doing?" he asked.

"We are fine. Doing just fine. So what are you taking next semester? I can't believe how fast this semester flew by."

"Definitely was an eye opener for my first semester." Trevor confessed. "Let's see, another math course. English literature 201, economics, speech, and American history."

"That sounds good, but you might have a lot of homework."

"It can't be worse than this semester's homework load." He chuckled. "I have eaten beans and rice for three months to save money for a new surfboard. And I plan on using it!" he told his mom.

"I have no doubt you will. So how is your job going?"

"It's good. Grocery store jobs are great to have. People pretty much leave me alone."

She sighed, "You always were a loner. But you need to be more social, Trevor."

"I know where your headed, mom. And yes one day you will have grandchildren." They had often had this conversation.

"Not if you continue to be a hermit crab."

"Yes, but people complicate my life."

"Yes, but our Christian walk is enriched and lived out on people."

"I know, mother." He cleared his throat. "It's just everyone is so weird and different out here. Makes me want to crawl in a hole."

"Like I said, hermit crab."

"Uggg. No kidding, but I am an *adult* mom."

Janet decided to drop the subject since Trevor was getting agitated. *He was right. He's an adult and I need to respect that.* They continued to talk until it was time for the bell to ring.

"Hey dude, how are you liking it here in the Golden state?" Trevor's co-worker asked.

"Man, I'm lovin' it." Trevor replied as he stocked the shelves.

His co-worker, Chastin, roared in laughter.

"What the heck?"

"You still got a thick southern accent. Where did you say you were from?"

"Tennessee."

"You mean … Teeeenaaaseee?" Chastin teased.

"It's not that bad, is it?"

"Oh yeah, it's bad. But I bet the chicks are diggin' it."

Trevor chuckled. "So that's why they keep asking me the same questions over and over. And here I thought they were deaf as a door post."

"Huh?"

"Oh nothing. Just another colloquial saying." He finished unloading his box and helped Chastin. "You going surfing today?"

"No way, dude. The surf is bumming."

Trevor shrugged his shoulders. "I guess I'm still so enamored with it. I go every chance I get. I haven't grown picky about my waves yet."

"Oh trust me, you will." Chastin said. "When the Santa Anna winds come … I bet you won't touch the ocean."

"Man, you are on!" Trevor slapped his back.

"So how is Ginger?"

"Uh, doing good. She's in fine shape."

"When are you going to see her next?"

"Just so happens today."

"Maybe I can meet this woman that has you smitten," Chastin said.

Trevor thundered in laughter. "You'll have to come out to Pismo Beach."

"What's so comical?"

"Ginger is the name of my short board!"

"Seriously, dude? You name your surfboards?"

"Well butter my butt and call me a biscuit. Guess you didn't see that one comin'?" Trevor told his new friend. "Yep. Just like in Tennessee, we named our animals on the farm."

"Man, how come I get the feeling we are like totally worlds apart?"

"Maybe you need to take a trip to the South … it is a place like no other."

"If that is true, why do you like living out here?"

"My dad was stationed at Vandenberg for eight years of his military career and I was in my formative years and fell hard for the ocean."

"And?"

"So after I graduated, I joined the military just like my dad. I served the hardest four years of my life. Believe me it was enough. I spent the last two of those years in Hawaii, where I learned how to surf and you could find me in the water every day, either before work or after work."

"Dude, why not go back to Hawaii?"

"I loved it there, but man it's too expensive. Besides, I wanted to go to college here. So I am right back where I used to live."

"So have you met any good looking chicks yet?"

"One thing is for certain, there ain't no muffin tops around here!"

"What?"

Trevor laughed. "I guess you would have no clue."

"I don't know what in the world you are talking about."

"In *the South*, they like fried chicken, fried green tomatoes, French fries, Pepsi, and a donut for dessert." Trevor chuckled at Chastin's facial expressions. "So do the math for a college student who sits all day. Oh plenty of beer on the weekend, while mudding in a vehicle."

"Okay … where do the muffins come in?"

"Now take that overweight chick and shove her into jeans two sizes too small, which shoves the belly up and over, then you cover it with a stretchy cling top."

"OOO … you are kidding me right? That sounds like totally gross. Do they not know what exercise is? Or like maybe grass juice. Let me guess … what do they consider, organic?"

"Oh you don't want to go there. For starters, there just isn't a market for it. You are not going to find a smoothie place, or a totally herb store. But I did see a sign up for R-GANIC eggs $2 a dozen once."

"Jeepers, are you for real?"

"They fry everything ... including butter!"

"That is like a heart attack waiting to happen, dude."

"Let's just say being a heart doctor in *the South* is a lucrative business."

They continued their conversation until Trevor clocked out and headed for his favorite place ... the ocean.

He tugged, stretched, and pulled until his wet suit was on. He ran toward the water, with his surfboard tucked under his arm, through the sand and crowd of people until he hit the foam and with one jump he was on top his surfboard paddling out.

As he took a wave, he balanced on top and felt Holy peace wash over him. He closed his eyes for a second and breathed in the salty air. *Oh Lord, You amaze me every time I get out in Your ocean. I am undone.* He continued to talk to his Lord as he surfed wave after wave. This was his happy place. His haven of complete peace with God and man.

Near dusk, he dragged himself out of the cold water. *Brrr.* He changed into some shorts and went home to fix some more beans and rice.

Trevor could not believe how fast the summer went by and now was sitting in his first week of the second semester at college. California has many strange and unusual sites. One of those being the crop fields. In the town he was living, they had huge strawberry fields. He had definitely sat and eaten his weight in the delicious red berry.

Because there were many huge strawberry fields, many field workers lived in this town. Their children were going to the same college as Trevor. It was the strangest thing. He was a white kid, a minority on campus, which actually played into his benefit.

The biggest area this showed up in was the English department. He was one of the very few students that could speak English well. Thus after his first week, he received an email which offered him a tutoring position in the English department. It would be a juggle, but he took it.

"Hi mom."

"Hi Trevor! So good to hear from you. I reckon you've been busy because I haven't heard from you lately."

"Yes, ma'am. I have been. I was offered a tutoring job in the English department."

"How awesome is that?"

"It's pretty cool. But between classes and my job, my surfing has suffered."

"Your surfing has suffered or you have suffered?"

"I admit; it's my happy place."

"That's not a bad thing, Trevor. So have you started your tutoring yet?"

"Yes. I have four students. This by far has been the easiest money I have ever made."

"So all those diagraming sentences helped, huh?"

"I guess so."

They talked of other things before she plunged into her important question. "You are coming home for Christmas right?"

Trevor cleared his throat. "I don't know how to say this, but no, I'm not. I am a poor student and don't have the money, and I don't want ya'll forking out the dough either. I'll be fine. I can always surf."

Janet closed her eyes to the onslaught of tears. She was silent for a bit before she could gather the courage to continue. They talked about family, siblings, and other pertinent information, but they did not broach the topic of coming home for Christmas again.

Trevor got out the flash cards he had made. He used a couple of catalogs, magazines, and the newspaper. He would point to the word. Then he would find a picture. Say the word three times. Then have the student point to the picture and say the word three times. Then at the end of the hour, he would quiz them by having them say the flash card word and find a picture for it.

His second student sat down in front of him. He patted his chest and said, "Trevor." Then he pointed to her.

She patted her chest and said, "Natalia."

They were well into the lesson when Trevor made a blunder. He patted his chest and said, "blunder."

She pointed to him, "Trevor?" she said with crinkled eyebrows.

Trevor could read confusion all over her face. He laughed. "Yes, Trevor. I messed up."

It was too hard to explain so he decided to continue the lesson. Trevor instantly connected to this girl. He had no idea why, but he couldn't deny the chemistry. He could not believe an hour had actually passed when his watch alarm went off. She stood and gave him a winning smile and left.

He shook his head; he was surely smitten. These college students knew most common English words. The hard part was sentence structure and comprehension. As he made new flash cards, he couldn't suppress the smile on his face.

He finished a full weekend of work. Then it was Monday and back at classes and tutoring. He hoped he could have a lot of surfing on the side.

Natalia came in as a graceful doe and sat opposite him.

"Trevor, hi." She attempted a greeting.

He laughed, "No it's, Hi Trevor."

"Hi Trevor, hope day is good."

"No it's I hope your day is good."

She was suddenly quiet. Trevor felt she didn't want to try for fear of correction. His heart went out to her. "Keep trying Natalia, you will get it."

She abruptly exhaled blowing her bangs. "I can't this English."

He had to hold back his snicker. "That's why I'm here to help you learn." He got out the flash cards and arranged them for her to pick and form a sentence.

She had placed the cards in this order A-dog-bite-man

"Okay, Natalia, let's add a few more. We are going to add *did* and *the.*"

He put them in the right places and then had her read: "A-dog-did-bite-the-man."

"See, that wasn't so bad. Now was it?"

He watched her head shake while he set up another sentence. "So Natalia, do you have many friends?"

"Friends?" she asked. Trevor nodded his head.

"Friends not I have."

"I do not have any friends," he corrected. She repeated after him and finally had a small laugh.

"Where are you from?"

"Russia."

"Oh, is your family here?"

"No, family still there."

He corrected her. "It's no, my family is still there."

She nodded.

"So how did you end up here on the Central Coast of California?"

"Students exchange."

"No say it this way. Exchange student."

He continued asking her questions and correcting her answers until his watch alarm went off. "What?" he said as he turned it off. "Boy, time goes by so fast with you."

"A boy named time?" she questioned.

He howled in laughter. She laughed after he explained. She gave her thanks and left. As he cleaned up he thought, *that was the best lesson yet.*

That day as he soared over the ocean foam, he got an idea. He planned to execute it the next week.

"Hi, mom." Trevor said over the phone.

"Hi, sweetie. How are ya?"

"I'm doing fantastic."

She noted his extra high-pitched voice. So she asked. "What's her name?"

"How did you know?"

"Remember when you were little and I told you I have eyes in the back of my head? They are still there!"

"Come on, mom, really, how did you know?"

"It's a mom thing. Now tell me her name. I'm most anxious to hear about this girl that has you awestruck."

"Well, there's not really much to tell. She's one of my tutoring students. She's from Russia and totally gorgeous, sweet, and kind."

"Well, now, I do believe she has put a spell on you."

"Oh, mom, I know it sounds crazy, but I'm hooked."

"Oh my, you got it bad, don't ya? You could always bring her home for Christmas," She hinted.

"Mom, we've been over this. Besides, I'm just getting to know her. If I bring her to *The South* she might think it's another planet."

"Just making a suggestion, son, that's all." Janet was disappointed that not only would her son not be home for Christmas, but she would not get to share in this part of his life.

Trevor changed the subject and they finished their call some 30 minutes later. Then Trevor rushed off to work.

"Hi Trevor," Natalia said as she sat down.

"Very good!" Trevor smiled. "And hi to you too."

Trevor plunged in right away. He gave her first set of cards to arrange. She put them this way: Me-with-out-you-go-will.

He laughed. "No, they go this way: will-you-go-out-with-me?" He read them out loud and looked at her soft creamy complexion for an answer.

"Oh," she covered her mouth and laughed. "Where out?"

He shrugged, "On a date."

"On a calendar?" she tilted her head.

He thought of how to explain. "Umm, no. Like you and me." He pointed. "Go to eat and then to a movie?"

He watched her cheeks go pink and she dipped her head. "Yes, that be good."

"That is good." He corrected. "When are you available?"

"Available?"

"When are you free?"

"When am I freedom?"

Trevor wasn't sure he was going to be able to contain himself. "Not freedom. When is a good time to pick you up for dinner and a movie?"

"Anytime," she said.

Trevor smiled. "You have to give me a day and time."

"Oh," she looked up. "Friday 5:00?"

Trevor finished their time with flash card arranging. When his timer went off, he received thanks and a winning smile before she left. "Ahh, this woman intrigues me. Never before have I fallen so quick or so blasted hard." He spoke to the empty room.

"Look, I really need you to fill in for me." Trevor implored Chastin.

"Dude, don't be messing with my Friday nights now."

Trevor slumped his shoulders in defeat and let out a big sigh.

"Oh alright. but this is the first and the last time I will fill in for you. There is a reason I am off on Friday nights – because I want to be."

"Got it man, I owe you one," Trevor said with a huge smile.

"Ah let me guess. It's a real girl?"

"Am I that easy to read?"

"Pretty much."

Trevor thanked him again and went about his work, planning for the next night.

He picked up Natalia and headed to his favorite hamburger joint. He ordered and then they sat down.

Trevor could tell she was nervous by the way she bit her lower lip.
"So tell me all about your country." Trevor said.

She had just begun when he stopped her. "Oops. That's our number. Hang on a second." He got up and got their tray.

"Wow, fries Frenchs everywhere!" she giggled.

Trevor howled. "Yes, they give a lot of French fries. That is how you say it."

"Lots of French fries."

"Yes. I dip them into ketchup." He did one to show her how.

She followed suit and wrinkled up her nose.

"So continue telling me about your country."

That was the start of a great evening. After they finished eating, they still talked … and talked … and talked. Trevor noticed that Natalia had relaxed.

Near dark, Trevor asked, "Would you like to stroll on the beach?"

"Beach?"

"Yes. Beach ... water." He motioned his arms like waves.

"Oh Yes. Big earth water bowl."

Trevor chuckled, threw away their trash, and headed to the closest beach.

They made it down to the water edge and Natalia stood and inhaled the salty air. He watched her close her eyes. Then she bent down and put her hands in the water.

"Cold, huh?" Trevor asked her.

She nodded and they walked along the edge and talked. Even through their language barrier, they never seemed to run out of words. When the time came, Trevor pointed in the direction of the sunset. Both watched in awe.

On the way to the car, Trevor stopped her. He grabbed her hand and said. "Natalia, you have been such a delight to be with. Thank you. I had the best evening ever."

She dipped her head in a slight nod while she bit her lower lip.

Trevor ran his fingers through his hair. "You want to do this again?"

She looked up ever so slightly and nodded yes.

Trevor let out a Yahoo, and continued to the car.

When Monday afternoon tutoring time came, Trevor couldn't quit smiling. Natalia was his third student. He thought she was more beautiful than ever.

"Hi, Trevor." She greeted as she took a seat opposite him.

"Hello, Beautiful." Trevor watched her cheeks heat.

"Before we start, Natalia. Let's pick a better date time. Friday nights I have to work."

"Umm," she pointed her slim finger to her chin. "Any calendar day is fine with me."

"So, did you like the beach?"

"Yes, the ocean bowl beach was best."

"Yes, the ocean bowl beach is the best. So can you go after class say on Tuesday and Thursdays?"

"Yes. That will be fine, Trevor, beach bum." She giggled.

Trevor ran his fingers through his hair and laughed. "Oh you ain't seen nothin' yet."

"Ain't?" she questioned.

"Oh my bad. That is Southern slang and you don't want to talk like that! I meant I love the ocean bowl so much I may as well be a fish."

"You fish swim like?"

"It's you swim like a fish," he corrected. "Oh yes. You'll see. But we better get on our lesson."

"Yes, and no south words."

Trevor laughed and started their lesson. Before he knew it, the timer buzzed. "I have one more student. If you wait in the library, we can go to the beach afterwards."

She agreed.

They parked and got out at yet another beach. This time Trevor was determined to do a little surfing. This was when he normally got to catch a wave or two. So babe or no babe, he was going to get some surfing first.

He took down his surfboard from his top carrier. "You don't mind if I surf for a few minutes do you?"

"Surf?" Natalia tilted her head.

"You don't know what surfing is, do you?"

She shook her head no.

"I will show you. But first, I am going to change in the bathroom." He normally just did the towel thing at his car, but with mixed company, the bathroom was a better choice.

Natalia cover her mouth in laughter. "You look funny. Why you wear bird suit?"

"Bird suit?"

"Little fat birds with white bellies in the Arctic?"

Trevor tilted his head and laughed. They continued to the water's edge as he explained why he used a wet suit. They watched several surfers while Trevor tried to explain the process. He clinched his teeth to keep from laughing at Natalia who was moving her body with every movement he explained.

He was just about ready to jump in when Natalia took his surfboard.

"Hey! What do you think you are doing?"

But his words were drowned out by the wind and crashing waves. She ran into the water, hopped on top the board and paddled out.

Trevor watched in sheer amazement. She knew exactly what to do. She curled into that wave like a pro. He shook his head. *"and all without a wetsuit!"* She surfed for nearly 40 minutes before getting out of the water.

She handed him back his surfboard. "Thanks, water bowl surf is, what do you say, cool?"

"Aren't you freezing?"

"Little"

He knew she was more than a little cold because her teeth were chattering and her fingers were turning blue.

"Where in the world did you learn to surf like that?"

"I told you, Trevor, I from Russia."

He grinned. "That's not what I mean. Let's get you to the car for a blanket."

Sitting in the car with the heater on, he asked her again.

"I learn to surf as a kid. My, what do you call helper for parent?"

"A nanny."

"Yes, nanny had a boyfriend who surfed. So we went to ocean bowl often. And well, he taught me and I would do it every chance I got."

"Why didn't you tell me?"

"I didn't know it important."

"Well, I guess it's not. Just you freaked me out back there! And how in the blazes of thunder did you do it without a wetsuit?"

"Blazes of thunder? I don't understand?"

"Oh never mind."

They were quiet for a moment.

"Are you disappoint me, Trevor?"

Her tone melted his heart. He took her hand in his. "No, I am not disappointed in you. I was worried about you. And really you knocked my socks off!"

"Where are they?"

He roared in laughter. "That is just a saying. I am super surprised!!"

He took her home. Before she opened the door, he cupped her chin and placed a kiss on her cheek. "I hope you know how special you are to me," he told her and left.

Their surfing connection seemed to bring together two very different cultures that were oceans apart. They became completely at ease with each other as though they had been friends for years. Not only so, but were gaining territory in the romance department. They spent every day they could together at the beach.

On the last day of the semester, Trevor handed her some index cards. "Put them in order Beautiful." He smiled, "Then answer me."

So she did. She put them like this: "Will you go with me to meet my parents for Christmas break?"

He waited for an answer.

"Are you sure like me they will?"

"Oh yeah, they will like you!" He opted not to correct her.

"I would be honored, Trevor, to go with you." She said carefully trying to place words correctly.

With that, he leaned over and indulged in finding her lips.

"Some lesson is this." She teased back.

"This is a lesson on love." He rubbed his chin. "I have tried not to be attracted to you, but I can't help it. Natalia. I am 100 percent head over heels in love with you."

She giggled. "Heads and heels?"

He wagged his finger. "I will explain at the beach later, but we might not get much surfing done.

A few weeks later on the airplane, Trevor laid his head on Natalia's shoulder. "You are so special to me. This Christmas will be the best ever."

"You, Trevor, are a crazy one."

"You ain't seen nothing yet."

They arrived in the wee hours of the morning and Trevor immediately put his plan into action. He squeezed Natalia's hand as they opened the front door of his parent's home. He quietly put on a pot of coffee. Then he took Natalia's hand and walked her to the entryway of the living room.

He put his figure to his lips when he saw her confused look. He squatted down and spread out some index cards. "Read them out loud."

"WILL YOU MARRY ME?" She squealed forgetting to be quiet. He pointed up and then kissed her with all the passion he had.

She was breathless when he finally pulled back. "What was that for?"

"A Christmas tradition that you must kiss if you stand under mistletoe. That's why my mom hangs it every year to see how many kisses she can get out of my dad."

She tilted her head and giggled. "Let me try mistletoe." She tenderly kissed Trevor. She placed a hand on Trevor's chest. "Trevor, the Lord had impressed my heart before I left my country that I not be going back. I cried. I was scared. But I trusted Him." She let a tear slip out. "I think this was why."

"Wahoo!" He yelled picked her up and swung her around.

"What in tarnation is all this noise about and on Christmas day to boot." He heard his mother say as she came down the stairs.

When she rounded the doorway and saw the intruders. She gasped, put her hand over her mouth as tears came streaming down.

"Oh my! You came home. Oh my joy is complete." She said and ran into her son's warm embrace. She pulled back and looked at his face. "I just can't believe it."

"Well mom, the only gift I brought is a soon to be daughter-in-law!"

"What?" she had nearly forgotten the woman standing in the room. She hugged her. Her son made the introductions.

"I see the mistletoe worked," his mom commented.

"Yes, mother, it did! Merry Christmas!"

The Christmas Card

The CD player went to the next song, *O Little Town of Bethlehem*. It had already played through three other Christmas carols while Sadie tapped her pen on the table. With tears streaming down her face, she put a slash through the next name. She took in a deep breath and continued addressing envelopes.

She grabbed her Christmas list when a sudden gush of wind nearly made it fly off the table. Her husband, Grant, came in the door with a load of wood under his arm.

He came to her when he disposed of the wood and took a seat across from her. "Oh boy, it's Christmas card time."

"Yeah," she slumped.

"Okay, what is it, sweetheart. I know that look."

"You know. It's the one name that haunts me every year. But I finally did it, Grant."

He raised his left brow, "Did what?"

"I marked her off. I can't keep going on like this!"

Grant took her hands into his. "Sweetie, these hands make the most wonderful cards ever. I know it takes a ton of work to make homemade cards. It's up to you. But you never know who you might be ministering to even if you never hear from them." He stood and kissed her on the forehead and wiped away a few tears and went back outside to cut wood.

Deck the Halls came on next and she went back to her envelope addressing. *"Lord, the pain is so great. Please help me to have joy. For You alone deserve all my praise and in You I put all my hope."* In no time, she was singing as she wrote in each address of people she had met all over the world. People who were near and dear to her heart.

Still sitting at the table ensconced in her task, Sadie allowed herself a break and watched her beloved husband steadily chopping wood for their wood burning heater. *He is such a good man,* but her thoughts didn't linger there. They went to where they always landed this time of year.

The year they moved across the United States to the golden state of California. For a southern girl, this was something akin to another planet altogether. She and her husband, devoted Christians, began in earnest to find a new church home. Though nothing was like the church family they had left, they did eventually settle into a conservative community church.

It is there that this story began. One Sunday soon after they had joined, Kayla and Mike introduced themselves to Grant and Sadie and invited them to lunch. They hit it off well with this couple. From that point on, the two women were inseparable.

They both had a love for rubber stamping and could often be caught spending hours making cards and laughing. Sadie shook her head at the precious memories that flooded her heart. She remembered the time when both of their kids had played dress up. Both her little boy and Kayla's little girl had dressed up as captains of a ship. The little ones were two peas in a pod.

Sadie and Kayla also did missionary events and women's retreats together. At almost any church function, these two worked behind the scenes. They took many walks to the park with the little ones, and, with the great weather on the coast, the two families often went to the beach together. Eventually they even began to do some camping adventures together. Sadie thought Kayla her best friend. Their friendship had taken off like kudzu … seven wonderful crazy years transpired then suddenly, there was a change.

Things in the church were difficult and Grant felt he and Sadie needed to move on. Nothing bad between the two families had transpired, but some other issues had come to the forefront and they made the decision to leave that church.

"I wonder if we had stayed … if it would have mattered?" she mused. She audibly sighed. *"Perhaps …"* She then allowed her mind to stray to the blow, to the horrifying wreck that hit her square in the face. *"I was so stupid!"*

The months that followed their church departure, Sadie had also begun a home business and was always swamped with work or schooling her three kids. There was little time left for cultivating new friendships with their new church family, much less maintaining old ones. So as time slithered rapidly away … so did Sadie and Kayla's bond. Not even seeing each other at church had a substantial negative impact on their floundering relationship.

Sadie, being mission minded, designed a mug and muffin Saturday morning Bible study. She had opted to make it community wide. That was when Sadie thought of Kayla and sent her an invitation. That was when the bomb fell.

Sadie received the ugliest return email. After several back and forth email conversations, it was quite evident to Sadie that Kayla was angry with her, but she had no clue as to why. They had never had a cross word with one another.

Thus, Sadie began the quest for answers. She brought bread by, she called, she emailed, and she even sent several cards begging for understanding. Finally, Kayla allowed Sadie to come by and see her. With tears streaming down her face, Sadie begged for Kayla to tell her what she had done wrong. Kayla wouldn't divulge her heart. However, something had gone awry. Sadie had done something horrific to have offended her dear friend in such a way. So Sadie did all she could and begged her friend for forgiveness for being too busy to do her part in the relationship.

Kayla, with tears in her eyes, said ... *NO!*

That day played over and over in Sadie's mind. She never understood what happened, but Kayla never talked to Sadie again. She ignored all contact from Sadie. Sadie prayed and prayed, but seemingly to a silent God. Six months later, Grant's job relocated and he moved their family to another region of the country. Never again to hear from their former friends.

A few names later, Sadie slammed her pen down. "I can't do it! I just can't do it." She said out loud to the CD player. She made a deal with the Lord. *"Okay God, IF I have one card left over I will send it to her. But if not, that will be my sign to let this go."* She went back to her ever-growing stack.

She worked hard until lunch. She had put on a Crockpot of chili early that morning. She whipped up some corn muffins and fetched her husband.

After a filling lunch, she went straight back to work. At four o'clock, she neared the end. Finally, to her amazement, she picked up the one remaining card and envelope. In disbelief, she checked back over her list to be sure she had not made a mistake. Sure enough, she had exactly one left over. She took in a deep breath. *"Okay Lord, You win."* She put Kayla and Mike Blanton Family along with their address on the last envelope, placed the handmade card, the family letter and picture in it. She put the hundreds of cards in a box to take to the post office the following Monday.

Though her friend was heavy on her heart, she chose to be cheerful for her husband. When he came in, she was singing with the CD player, *Walking in a Winter Wonderland*.

"Someone is in a good mood," he smiled at his wife and kissed her.

"Why not? There is so much to be merry about."

"You could have fooled me this morning." He said with his left eyebrow raised.

"You are not going to believe this, but I told God that IF I had one card left over I would send it to Kayla. And He did the darnest thing."

"What's that?"

"I had exactly one left over." She shrugged. "So Monday morning, it's in the mail … *again*."

Grant wrapped his arms around his wife, "I am proud of you."

"For what?"

"For being you," he said and tapped her on the nose.

Sadie had her Christmas oldies blaring as she pulled into the post office parking lot. She turned off her car then put her hand over the box and prayed for the people who were going to receive these cards. Then she did as she had been doing for the past 4 years. She pleaded for a certain card.

"Lord, just maybe this will be the year?" she pleaded her cause before the Lord. She went in and did the long duty of putting a postage stamp on each card. When that was complete she handed them to the postmaster and headed home with a joyful heart.

She had gingerbread cookies in the oven when her husband came home.

"Hmmm, what is that yummy smell wafting to my nose? Must be the consequences of these precious hands," He told his wife as he kissed the palms of each hand.

"You are going to make us late for the Christmas play practice."

He raised his eyebrows. "Not me!"

After two full weeks of play practice, it was the night of the play. Now they were at home. "Oh Grant, I never tire of Christmas! The redemption party of a life time … it never gets old to me!" She hugged him, "Tonight was a lot of work, but it is always worth it."

"I completely agree with you." He said as he took off his tie. "You, my little jewel bug, need some rest."

Sadie had just slipped her nightgown over her head. "It would be perfect if only …"

Grant pulled the hair out from around her neck. "Remember, we don't do *if onlys*. We talk about this every year. You cannot make amends or changes or even apologize if the person offended does not tell you the grievances."

"I know. But I still long for reconciliation." She said as she slipped her feet into the cold sheets.

"If God had given us stone hearts we wouldn't care and we wouldn't do His mission." He turned out the light.

Sadie pulled one pan of cookies out of the oven and popped in another one. She was baking for her husband's office gifts and her neighbors. She had three more batches to go. She stretched her aching back and closed her eyes.

She jerked her eyes opened at the sound of the phone. "Who could it be now? Today would not be a good day for sales calls. I am up to my elbows in dough."

She hurriedly picked up the phone, "Hello," she said breathlessly.

"Hi Sadie."

"Kayla!?" she screamed in the receiver.

"First I want you to know I read and kept every Christmas card you sent me. I have been under conviction for over a year now to make amends. Can you forgive me for letting this go this long?"

"I just want to know what did I ever do to hurt you."

"You know, let's just move on. Merry Christmas, Sweet Sadie." Kayla said.

Sadie swallowed hard. She desperately wanted to know but she let her friend take the lead. "Oh Kayla how I have missed you. I can't think of a better time than the season of redemption that makes forgiveness possible."

The batch of cookies burned! The gifts she was working on were left unfinished for another day while two best friends redeemed their lost relationship, the true meaning of Christmas.

The Mysterious Jingler

"Thank you, Merry Christmas." (ring ring) "Thank you, Merry Christmas." Calvin blew on his hands. "Merry Christmas to you too, ma'am." He didn't let the rolling eyes or the rejection keep him from wishing everyone a Merry Christmas.

"And you, too, little one. Thank you and may you have a very Merry Christmas!"

"Aren't you cold?" the lady asked as she dropped a few coins in his red hanging bucket.

"Ahh, it is for a good cause, ma'am." She agreed and went into the store.

Calvin was indeed cold, but his warm heart melted for people in need so he kept ringing his bell.

"God bless you, ma'am. Thank you sir." The day passed quickly as he greeted smiling faces and some that weren't smiling. Now it was time to pack up.

Calvin was into his third day when *Miss Prim &* *Proper* came by. He had greeted her every day as she arrived for work only to have an offensive grimace returned. "And Merry Christmas to you." He had to grit his teeth not to get a bad attitude. Instead, he prayed for her.

It was an exceptionally cold day. Snow was falling along with the temperatures. Still Calvin jingled on. The manager of the Christian store came out to tell Calvin they would be closing early. Calvin thanked the man and took the opportunity to get the worker, *Miss Prim & Proper's* name. He jotted a message on a piece of paper and asked the manager to give it to her.

At the close of the store, Calvin watched for the girl. When he spotted her, she was not coming his way. Though disappointed he still called after her.

She turned and stomped her way to him. "You are embarrassing me! What do you want?"

Taken aback Calvin spoke, "I beg your pardon. Did you not get my message?"

"Yes I got your message, but ..." she looked around.

"Oh, I get it. You don't want to be seen with the likes of me." He gritted his teeth. "Real Christian like!"

"Look, mister, just because it's a Christian based store does not mean all the workers are Christian." She waved her hand in the air. "I'm not saying I'm not a Christian. People do a mighty lot of assuming these days."

He chuckled, "Yes they do. Including you."

"What are you accusing me of?" She snorted as she tightened her scarf against the icy wind.

Calvin tried to be nice. "Just seems the judgments of assumptions go both ways."

"Well, whatever. I need to get out of this bad weather. So what is it you wanted?"

He raised his eyebrows. "Well I had wanted to take you to dinner to talk about just such topics."

He watched her eyes look him over. His heart sank. *When will people learn …*

She cleared her throat. "It's getting pretty nasty our here. Umm. Maybe another time." As quick as her boots would let her, she rushed to her car and was gone.

That night after dinner, Calvin lay reading his Bible. He had to be so very careful with his thoughts. He decided to just pray them.

Father, You know how very much I struggle with this. It is so wrong. To judge people by appearances is so against what You stand for. Yet in my aggravation and justification of it, I don't want to sin by rebutting with a judgmental attitude. Father, our world is so broken, yet You love us anyway!

He pulled his tattered blanket tighter and adjusted his hat. He continued to talk to his Father until he fell asleep.

It was eight days before Christmas when he saw Rachel again. This time he caught her as she walked to the door.

"Good morning and Merry Christmas, Rachel." He told her as he rang his little bell.

She said hi with a grimace.

"Hey how about dinner when you get done with work?"

She sighed. "You probably aren't going to leave me alone until we do this, are you?"

"Umm, probably not." He said with a smile.

"Fine. I get off at five."

"Great. I'll be ready."

He watched her roll her eyes and go into the store. He prayed not only for her, but also for himself that he would not get angry at the judgments of so called "*anti*-judging people."

His prayer brought back his good spirit. "Thank you, sir." (ring ring) "Thank you, sweetie." (ring ring) "Every bit helps, thank you." (ring ring) "You're making a difference, thank you."

The day flew by. Five pm arrived and Rachel walked out the door.

"You ready?" Calvin asked.

"As ready as I'll ever be." She grumbled. "Where to?"

"How about McDonalds?"

"Why, is that all your bucket will buy you?" she muttered.

Whoa, pretend you didn't hear that! Ignoring her comment, he asked, "Is the one on Calhoun Road good for you?" He began to disassemble is tripod. "Do you mind waiting until I get this in my car?"

"I will just meet you there." She uttered and left.

Calvin worked as quickly as his freezing hands would move. He shook his head. He had a feeling she wasn't even going to show up. No-shows were common in his world. He was pleasantly surprised when he saw her car outside McDonald's. With a deep breath, he went inside. She was waiting just inside the door.

He ushered her to counter. "Please order first," he told her.

"Okay, but I will get my own, thank you."

Calvin sighed. She was making this difficult but he didn't want to fight her. "What? You don't think I have enough in my *bucket* for the both of us."

"I don't eat from stolen money." She whispered over her shoulder. Then she ordered and paid for her meal.

Calvin rubbed the back of his neck while he restrained his words. He stepped up and ordered.

They sat down across from one another. Calvin bowed his head and prayed silently. He opened his eyes to see the wide eyes of his meal partner.

"Normally, when on a first date ..." Calvin began but was cut short.

"Let's get this straight, this is *not* a date."

"Okay, on this first conversation, we would ordinarily talk about our work, lives, and aspirations. However, it seems like we have a judging contest going on. Perhaps we should just clear the air first."

He noticed he had grabbed her attention. "So Miss Rachel. It is Miss right?"

She nodded.

"What has gone through your mind about me? You evidently have some opinions." He could hear her switching her feet under the table.

She cleared her throat. "I will be brutally honest with you."

"Please do." He encouraged.

"I think you were here last year. You guys come and prey on *Christian* stores because you think you will get more money out of *Christian* customers. I think you all are frauds, that you just take the money for yourself. I think that is despicable."

Calvin let out a low whistle. "That certainly explains the looks. You mentioned that, just because it was a Christian store, doesn't mean everyone who works there is a Christian. Well, not every Jingler is a crook. I personally take great offense to your description. I stand out in the freezing cold, in all kinds of elements, and give EVERY cent to the represented foundation. It is one way I can help those in need."

He ignored her raised eyebrows. "You probably don't have an inkling on just how cold it gets out there."

"Not really."

Calvin took a deep breath and calmed himself before he continued in a quiet voice. "People need to quit judging a book by its cover, but open it up and read it. Try getting to know that person or walk a day in their shoes."

She nodded. "I agree with that."

He took a chance here. If he sounded preachy, it would defeat his purpose. "Better yet, open up The Book, The Bible and read it."

"So you are a believer?"

"Yes. I bet this surprises you too. Let me guess ... no Jingler *crook* can be a Christian?" His eyes twinkled, but he was trying to get his point across.

"I am sorry. It's just that there is so much fraud. It seems everyone wants money, especially at Christmas time. And you know, like they showed on that news station about the homeless being really well-to-do people living off a cardboard sign."

Calvin really needed wisdom to handle this carefully. "Again, instead of making one swooping statement about the whole library, take each book off the shelf read it and then you might be more qualified to make a judgment." He snickered. "The news, and the info-torials are very slanted at best."

"You're probably right." She smiled. "Lesson learned, I think anyway."

Calvin's heart did a "YES!" she gets it. "So tell me Rachel, are you a believer?"

Her eyes told him what he needed to know. "Yes. I am." She paused. "I don't know the Bible very well. But I am learning."

"Good. Read your Bible, pray, and obey." He encouraged her. "I know. It's easy to say, much harder to do."

"No kidding. AND keep your foot out of your mouth." She laughed.

Now that he had peeled off her bristly outer coating, he was enjoying this fresh new convert. They went on to talk about other topics, including the different ministries each was involved in before departing and going their separate ways.

The next day when she came to work she bobbed up to the Mysterious Jingler with a smile and dropped some money into his bucket.

"Good morning and Merry Christmas, Rachel! By the third day, he got up enough nerve to ask her back to McDonalds. "And we don't have to call it a date."

"Sure. I'll be there. Have a great Jingley day." She said as she bounced inside to work.

A form of these *not* dates continued though the week. On Christmas Eve when Calvin went through the dinner line, his eyes bulged out and he pulled the bill of his cap lower. The person passing out the dinner rolls was none other than Rachel.

That was close. "Thank you," he said and tried to hurry away.

Immediately Rachel gasped. "Mr. Jingler?" she went around the stack of trays. "Is that you?"

Oh boy here goes. There was no stopping the inevitable. "Hi Rachel, what are you doing here?"

"I was going to ask you the same question." She pointed to her apron. "I'm serving."

"And I'm eating. Thanks so much."

Calvin could see a thousand questions swim across her face, but there was more people in the line so he watched her go back to serve. He determined to finish eating by the time the last person was through the line. He didn't think she was ready to know the *real* Mysterious Jingler.

And so it was. Christmas came and went. The Mysterious Jingler managed to escape the scrutiny of Rachel. After the last encounter, Calvin found himself always looking for her car before entering the city homeless shelter. For some reason, he could not get this girl out of his mind and he didn't want her to see him there.

So he prayed. *Lord, there is no way this girl would ever understand much less love a guy like me. So if she is not for me can You please, erase her from my memory. Even above love, I want Your will.*

January came with a vengeance. On more than one occasion, Calvin felt like throwing in the towel, but then he had actually started bonding with a few folks. He knew making a difference would be a very slow and arduous process.

For over a year now, Sunday was his only normal day. He actually went to his church mission house where he showered, dressed for church, and talked with the mission team and staff of the church that was sponsoring him on this mission project.

He also knew where Rachel attended church. So on this particular Sunday, he got up enough nerve to do it. When Rachel approached her car, Calvin was leaning against it. She covered her mouth.

"What are you doing here?"

"Freezing to death," he teased. He actually was having trouble looking away. He wanted to soak in that precious face.

"You're such a tease," she tapped him on the shoulder. "Really what brings you to this part of town?" Her eyes sparkled which gave him the courage to tell her.

"To be for sure, it was to ask you out on a *not* date. To somewhere *not* McDonald's.

With her hands on her hips, she asked, "Really?"

"Yes, really."

"Umm, yeah, okay. I have been worried about you. You pop up in the most mysterious places."

"My car?" He questioned.

She put a finger to her cheek.

"You're not still afraid of me are you?"

"Are you kidding? No."

"Then right this way, ma'am." So he escorted her to his modest car. It was old but clean and it served its purpose, taking him to and from work, when he worked. As he drove they entered into easy conversation. It was as though they picked up right where they left off. A deep bond was developing at a lightning rate. Calvin had to fight the feeling that they were meant to be together.

He could still hear Rachel's laughter as he bundled up against the elements. They had spent the entire day together. He chuckled as he remembered her reaction when he pulled into a Burger King and told her this was *not* McDonald's. They spent hours getting to know each other.

That night, as he clicked off his flashlight, he said, *I think I love her! But it would never work. Go to sleep and just forget it.*

Though his mind told him one thing, his heart argued. So what started out as a fun Sunday *not* date, turned into a very delightful routine. Each week, they grew closer and closer. It was too cold to walk for long stents, but they would bundle up and walk. On this particular day, their gloved hands touched and Calvin slipped his into hers and looked into her face for approval. Wisps of her golden hair framed her face as she smiled at him.

Later when he took her home and said good night, he grabbed her hand in his. "I had to know if it was as soft and beautiful as it felt through your gloves."

Rachel gasped.

Calvin switched his feet. "Rachel," he brushed her check with the back of his hand. "I think I am falling fast."

"Yeah, me too," she whispered.

Then he left. He knew he was dancing with fire and he would likely get burned, but he just couldn't help himself. He was in love with Rachel. He would cross each bridge as it came.

He had been very careful not to be at the shelter when Rachel volunteered. But what he didn't expect was that she would appear at his *house* with a bag of groceries. He watched her give away bags along the alleyway. He scrunched down and huddled under his blanket as far as he could.

"Here, sir. I brought you some food." She knelt down. "I also have some water, and toiletries." When she reached for the blanket, she muttered, "Calvin?" As the blanket gave way, so did Calvin's secret.

He watched her cover her mouth, back away and then she turned and ran. He could hear her gasps as she ran from the nightmare he knew would happen one day. *What was I thinking! That she would fall for a homeless guy?*

There was no need to run after her. Not only was he out of food, but out a woman that had become very dear to him. He closed his eyes. He needed prayer.

Sunday came. He didn't bother to meet her at her car, which had become a delightful habit. He went back out on the streets though a little piece of his heart was missing. Though it was April, a cold wind cut through his street clothing. *Lord, I need Your strength and Your vision to make it through today.*

Spring turned to summer. Summer fell into fall. Fall slipped into winter. Calvin never forgot Rachel. He thought he would never forget her. He hadn't really ever experienced love before and it made him do some thinking. He knew it was too late for Rachel, but if that should ever happen again, would he be willing to give up his street ministry? It was crazy to entertain the thought of bringing a bride home to your three-level cardboard box.

All of these things swirled through his mind as he set up his red tripod and got out his bell. He couldn't help hoping that he would get a glimpse of Rachel if she still worked at this store.

"Thank you sir." He smiled, "Merry Christmas." (ring ring) "Thank you, little one. Merry Christmas." He continued to smile and be joyful the entire day.

It was the third day when he spotted Rachel walking toward the store. He rang his bell extra loud. "Merry Christmas, Miss!" He received exactly was he expected ... an eye rolling scowl. Calvin sighed. He said a prayer, took a deep breath, and continued to do his volunteer work as unto his Lord, but his heart of flesh was breaking.

"Merry Christmas!" (ring ring) "Thank you, Merry Christmas." Calvin rubbed his gloved hands together. He thought, *should I or should I not? She probably wouldn't. He tilted his head, but then again if she did ...* He decided that, in the next lull of customers, he would do it.

At lunchtime, he had several employees offer to bring him lunch. He turned them down, but did ask one of them to take Rachel a note. He was hopeful as he continued to ring his bell. Then when the second wave of lunch breaks hit, Rachel came out holding the note and walked up to him. Calvin felt the air leave his chest.

"This is like de ja vu. I mean you're right again. I judged a book by its cover." She looked away. "I was just so so, umm. I felt lied to, deceived. I mean you coming on Sunday's in a suit and all. Then to see you so so ..."

"Homeless," he filled in. "Rachel, look at me." He waited for her to comply. "Believe me I never ever wanted to hurt you. If you give me a chance, I can explain."

"That's why I'm here. I don't know if I can get over the lies, but as a believer, I owe you the opportunity to explain."

Calvin let out a big sigh. "Can we do McDonald's after work?" he asked, his eyes begging for understanding.

"Sure." She said and walked off.

When she returned from her lunch break. She brought him a tall cup of hot chocolate. "Thank you," he whispered. He was touched at her caring.

Just as had happened exactly one year prior. They drove separate vehicles to McDonald's. They each ordered and took a seat opposite each other.

Calvin began. "Well, there is no sense in small talk. I will get right to the issue at hand. "Yes, I'm homeless and no, I'm not homeless."

"Come on Calvin, explain this mystery." She said as she tapped on the table.

Calvin drew in a deep breath. "I've been doing street ministry for about two years. Like you, I had been doing occasional ministry at the shelter, but I felt I was ineffective. These "street" people, if you want to call them that, are just as real and important as you and I. Therefore, I knew that if I really wanted to reach them, I would have to earn their trust enough to show them Jesus. The only way I could see that happening is if I became one of them."

He rubbed the back of his neck. "So I talked with our church staff and they agreed to pay me a very small stipend and let me shower and dress on Sunday mornings in the mission house at the back of the property. But otherwise, I am just like everyone else the other six days a week."

"Wow! Are you kidding me?"

"No. But I must tell you that I had not considered the prospects of marriage when doing this arrangement." He raised his eyebrows. He sure hoped she would understand.

"It's a lot to take in. I just freaked out when I saw you. I was so shaken that I just couldn't process it."

"But even after you saw me this morning you did not try to address it. Why?"

She shrugged. "I guess old habits die hard."

"Yes, which is the very reason I'm so adamant about giving the discarded people a voice. My goal is to distinguish people's myths and injustices about the homeless."

"That is such a huge undertaking."

"It is. I can't say it doesn't have some major draw backs."

"Like?"

"For one, what people think of me, especially a certain young lady that I had become very fond of." He knew he was placing his raw heart on the table for her to crush if she so desired, but what else did he have to lose?

She studied his face a moment. "I didn't know this whole Christian thing would be so hard. I find myself having to relearn things."

He nodded.

"So, umm. Do you actually have a job?"

"Yes and no." He chuckled. "I work three days a week as a mechanic. It has been amazing to me just how many do work jobs. It's just not enough to keep a roof over their head. If I have learned one thing, it is that walls and a roof are the only differences. If you were to peel back the roof and walls in any given subdivision, middle to upper class, you would find the people are the same. The only thing that separates them is sheetrock and an address."

"Wow!" she said. "So what are your plans?"

Calvin felt his entire future depended on this one conversation. Would she understand? Could he really ask her to share his life as it was at that moment? After a quick prayer, he answered. "Depends."

"On what?"

"On you."

"On me? Why me?"

Calvin cleared his throat. "I guess I should ask if you are seeing anyone."

"No." she fidgeted in her seat.

"Are you going to ditch me again or let me work through this?"

"Now that you have explained everything. I uh, think we uh …" She laughed, "I don't know what I am saying yes to!"

"How about to just follow God's lead and see where He takes us?"

"Yes. That's it exactly."

The next day Calvin watched a smiling Rachel approach. He greeted her with, "Merry Christmas!"

"And merry Christmas to you, too!" She gave him a cup of coffee and a muffin. "Have a great day, my mysterious Jingler."

He laughed. "Thank you for the treats. Hey by the way, how did you know it was me?"

"The gloves silly." She said over her shoulder as she tossed her hair.

Calvin's heart swelled as he watched her walk into the store.

On Christmas Eve, Calvin knocked on Rachel's door. Her dad answered.

"Can I help you?"

"Uh Yes. Is Rachel home?"

"Yes. May I ask who you are?" The older man asked.

"Tell her it's the Mysterious Jingler."

After a moment's scrutiny, he turned and called Rachel.

She came out on the porch and shut the door. "Hey Calvin. What brings you here?"

He thought he would melt under her stare. "Oh yeah, well, uh, here." He handed her a little box and said, "Merry Christmas, Rachel!"

"Oh, Calvin you didn't have to give me anything."

"Rachel," he put a hand on her cheek. "I don't think you know how much you mean to me."

They were caught in each other's gaze until Calvin finally cleared his throat. If he wasn't careful, he was going to lose his head. This whole *love thing* had his heart spinning out of control! "Well, I better go."

"We were just sitting down to eat, please join us." she pleaded.

Calvin rubbed the back of his neck. "I can't, Rachel. I made a vow to God on this and I can't break my promise." This was much harder than he ever dreamed it would be.

"Hey, I got an idea. Wait right here." She flew back inside her house. Then she stuck her head back out the door. "It's cold out there. Why don't you come in and wait."

He winked at her, "You know why. I will wait out here. Oh but thank you."

He whistled, he prayed, and he waited. Then in a snatch of time, she was back out, her arms loaded. "Here take these." She said and went back inside. She came out with more.

"What on earth are you up to?" Calvin asked.

"We're going to take Christmas Eve dinner to your place." She said as she wrapped a scarf around her coat and put on her gloves.

"You are amazing! Do you know that?"

"I don't know about all that amazing stuff. Where's your car?" she asked.

"Umm, I only use it on Sundays to come see you," he confessed.

With her hands on her hips she spoke,. "Talk about amazing … I think I'm looking at one amazing man of God." She went back in and grabbed her keys. "We'll take my car then."

They loaded everything up and went back toward down town. Calvin was humbled. *Lord, I so don't deserve this woman!*

After they had passed out all but one plate, they sat down in Calvin's *home* and shared the best Christmas Eve dinner ever, not so much because of the food but because of the company.

"You, Miss Rachel Aldridge, have made me the happiest most blessed man on earth tonight." He looked into the eyes of the woman he loved and wondered if she could love him back.

He laughed when he heard Frank say *me too*, along with Jimmy, Sonny, and Trevon. "There is sure no privacy here." He whispered.

"Isn't this what Christmas is all about?" she said.

"Yes."

They simply stared at one another. The moon gave Calvin just enough light to see her lips. "Tell me if this is unwanted." Before she could ask, "What?" His lips brushed hers. He did not hear anything but a sweet gasp, so he tried again, thinking his ears deceived him. Only this time he lingered a little longer.

"Oh my," she said as she shivered.

"Rachel, you better get home, but if my advances are not welcome, you need to let me know now. Because, I am falling fast. No I take that back, I'm completely fallen."

"I fell a long time ago," she confessed. "I just haven't admitted it even to myself.

"Oh Rachel! I never knew love could turn your world upside down." He wanted to kiss her again. Actually, he wanted to kiss her all night long. Instead, he stood and held out his hand to help her up. He walked her to her car.

"I love you Rachel." He kissed her passionately.

"I love you, my mysterious Jingler," she said and left.

At about 11:00 Christmas morning, Calvin was awakened by the smell of coffee and cinnamon rolls. "Hey there sleepy head. Merry Christmas."

Calvin thought his grin would freeze in place. "I certainly could get used to waking up like this every morning."

"Umm, me too. Yeah. Come on now," were words coming from surrounding boxes and voices.

By then just about everyone in the alley was surrounding Calvin and Rachel. "Well let's get this thing rolling. Merry Christmas, everyone!" Rachel said then she pulled out coffee cups. She had brought several carafes of coffee, and a pan of homemade cinnamon rolls. She served all that. "So guys give me about 15 minutes ... and I will have some hot soup ready."

They all thanked her profusely and went to their own *cardboard pad*.

"You are a sight for sore eyes!" Calvin stared at her.

"What? What's wrong?" she asked thinking she had food stuck in her teeth.

"You that's all, just you!"

"Stop it or you will have me in a puddle!" she said. "And besides, 15 minutes will go by fast." She handed him his Christmas gift.

"You didn't have to get me anything. Just being with you has me over the moon." He carefully unwrapped the small box. Inside was a bell with a black handle. He read the engraving that swirled around the edge.

> *To the Mysterious Jingler who taught me*
> *To never judge a book by its cover, but*
> *To open its pages and read within!*
>
> *Love Rachel*

"I don't know what to say Rachel!" He swallowed the lump in his throat. "Thank you. It is precious beyond words."

"I think it's interesting that you got me an elegant bell necklace, and I got you a unique bell. Either we are both ding-a-lings, or we were both thinking of how we met."

He tapped her on the nose. "I think you're right." As Calvin guessed, his neighbors began arriving. He stood and helped her up. "Let's serve Christmas, my sweet Rachel."

The weeks following were filled with duel ministering. It wasn't every day. The nights that followed the days that Rachel came out and really got to know his people were often sleepless. Rachel often brought soup or sandwiches. She always brought some kind of sweets she had made. But more than that, she gave her heart to these *lesser thans by the world's standards.*

As love does … the Sunday before Valentine's Day when Rachel walked out of church to her car she was in for a great surprise. For there in front of her car, Calvin had his tripod and bucket set up. He was ringing his bell and he held a cardboard sign. She read:

Will you marry me?

The Cookie Crumbs

"Okay, okay, just one." Claire held the plate as steady as her feeble hands could. "You little stinker, I saw you take two." she said to the little boy. She moved the plate around to the rest of the kids.

"Do you have Kool-Aid, too?" a kid asked, wiping crumbs from his face.

"What is the special word?" she asked the group.

"Please," came a disjointed chorus from the neighborhood kids.

"Aren't you cold?" she asked the little girl that was barley clothed for the winter weather.

The little girl didn't answer but grabbed a cookie and darted away. Claire's heart broke. It wasn't the first time her heart had broken over a child that was either cold, hungry, abused, or unloved.

She served some Kool-Aid and then offered the kids another round of cookies before they hurried off.

As she watched them run off, she prayed for each one. She got out the broom and swept off the cookie crumbs. *"Lord, help me to love them."*

Two days later, she was up to her elbows in dish suds when the banging began. She quickly dried her hands and went to the door. Yet another group of kids were at her door.

"Got any cookies for us?" one child asked.

"Sure, sweetie," she answered. "Anyone want some hot cocoa, too?"

Their shouts made Claire smile. She prepared the treats then took them out to the shivering children. She had been worried the first winter when she saw how often and how long the kids stayed out of doors. She had just handed out the last cup of hot chocolate when two boys began a fight.

"Now, boys, remember what I said?" She separated them. "Not around my house. Besides, it's not nice to fight. Don't forget that God is watching you all the time."

"Okay," the boys reluctantly quit, though she was sure they would probably duke it out as soon as they were out of her sight.

Claire smiled at the hot cocoa mustaches they had before darting off to play. As she swept the cookie crumbs off her porch, she prayed for each child. Their names had been challenging to memorize but she had finally managed.

When she went back to her dishes, she thanked the Lord for giving her this opportunity to share His love to these kids. She couldn't believe she'd been there 12 years.

"Hey, Betsy, sorry I'm late." Claire said as she took a seat at the bagel shop.

She waved her hand. "No worries. I know things come up."

They both ordered and settled in the cozy booth for fellowship and prayer.

"So, how was your week?" Betsy asked as she smothered her bagel with rich cream cheese.

"Oh about the same. I live a fairly boring life. But the assignments God sends to me, well, they are quite lively!" Claire laughed. "It never ceases to surprise me how much the kids roam outside even in the dead of winter."

"Oh dear, that sounds crazy."

Claire shrugged. "That is how they live in the low income housing section of town. Not all, but many of the kids come from who knows where. Some live in such bad conditions I shudder."

Betsy reached over and touched Claire's hand. "That is why God sent them you!" She brushed away a tear. "You are the safe haven right in the middle of the wars that rage behind closed doors."

"It's not easy." Claire sighed. "Not easy at all." She bit into her bagel with delight. She didn't often get such a delicacy.

"I can only imagine." Betsy said. "I couldn't handle the anytime cookie jar, much less the children themselves."

Claire raised an eyebrow. "It took me some wrestling with God, but He finally convinced me it is all His time, and that is the way it is over there. I suppose, that as long as God keeps the oil aflowin' I'll be abakin' cookies!"

Betsy tilted her head. "Huh?"

"You know the story of the widow's oil that never ran dry? Well, it has been so amazing to me how God has kept me in flour, chocolate chips, and butter!" She shook her head. "I don't know how He does it, but when I run low, someone gives me a donation, or I find a bag of cookie supplies on my door step. Or friends like you bring me hot chocolate and cups." She swallowed past the lump in her throat. "As long as God keeps me in *oil*, I will keep sweeping cookie crumbs off my porch."

"That sure is a modern day Bible story if I ever heard one." Betsy smiled into her friend's eyes. "Do tell me though, it has gotten better over the years right?" Betsy asked.

"Yes and no," Claire said with a grin.

Betsy wrinkled her forehead. "What do you mean?"

"Well, by the time I get a group of kids not to steal my clothes off the clothesline, or to stop breaking my herb pots, stomping my flowers, you name it, they are gone and there's another group to train." She chuckled at the recollection.

Betsy shook her head. "Are you serious?"

"Yes. I mean, I had to bite my tongue once when I saw two boys rolling around on the ground in my bed sheets off the line."

Betsy had to hold in her laughter.

"Yeah, you laugh." Claire smiled. "In retrospect, I can laugh about it, but at the time, I was so angry I had to calm down before I could go outside. By then the boys were gone. But they had grass stains all over the sheets, mud from their feet and, you guessed it, dog pooh too."

"All I can say is, God knew what He was doing by placing you there and not me."

"I never would have dreamed that I would be living in housing authority duplexes when I was younger. But that is how God changes us to be more like Him." She sipped her coffee. "See my house is a palace, Betsy."

"A palace? You've got to be kidding?"

"No. I'm not. God can make anything a palace. Because He is there with me, it is a palace. He has made it beautiful to me. I love it!"

Betsy was humbled yet again by spiritual *crumbs* from the *cookie* lady. "You are such an inspiration, Claire."

"Don't get me wrong. I still sin. I still struggle. Like last year when I had worked my fingers to the bone making all those sock snowmen only to find some of them torn apart and strewn down the sidewalk."

"Oh my. So sorry."

"That really hurt my feelings. But I have to remember, that while I was yet a sinner Christ died for me." She smiled. "That one reminder keeps me going. And when it gets hard, or I think I can't do it anymore, God sends me a *golden carrot*, a spiritual incentive, if you will."

"A *golden carrot*? Betsy questioned.

"Like when one of the girls came to me and asked for help when her momma was shot. Or the little boy who would sneak out to my house for me to read him Bible stories. Another example, the one young teen girl that came almost daily to talk. She came for at least two years. I don't know if these kids will even remember me. Or if they ever retain anything thing I tell them about Jesus, but I hope so."

"There is no doubt that these kids will remember the arms of love from your cookies and the crumbs that come with it." Betsy wiped at a tear. "Shall we pray for those little rattails right now?"

Claire printed a message inside of each book then carefully wrapped it. Along with 10 dozen cookies bundled six to a bag, Claire was set to make her rounds. She went to each house that had one of her *cookie* kids. She hugged, squeezed, and wished each one a Merry Christmas! By the time she pulled her red wagon back to the house, she was exhausted. She brushed cookie crumbs free from her apron and took it off. She fell asleep right there on the couch.

She awoke Christmas day to banging on her door. *That's strange. Kids don't usually come on Christmas day.* She said to herself as she opened the door and stepped outside. "Can I help you?"

There stood on her sidewalk a young man with a baby on his hip and a poinsettia in his other hand. His smile revealed all his teeth. He walked towards her. "I hope so. You got a cookie?"

"Yes," she said slowly. Confusion wreaking havoc in her head.

The young man began to laugh. "Mrs. Claire, it's Romano. You remember me?"

Recognition hit her full force. "You mean the rug rat eight-year-old Romano that dug up every flower I had? The boy that used to take delight in scaring me to death with spiders and lizards? The kid that always took more than his share of cookies? Surely you are not the same Romano that cut holes in my husband's t-shirts?"

He hung his head for a moment and then looked the old lady in the eye. "Yes ma'am. It is the same Romano, only different. See you thought I wasn't listening to your Bible stories, but I was. After I moved from here through my teen years I did some real dumb stuff, but I always remembered you and how much you loved this Jesus person. So when I hit bottom, I found I needed this Jesus you spoke of. And here I am a changed man!"

Claire through her arms around him, baby and all. "Hallelujah!"

"Oh and this is for you." He handed her the live poinsettia. A note was tied to it.

"And who is this?" She inquired about the baby as they went into her house.

"This is my daughter, Azonia. I am married and my wife is a believer too."

Claire put her hand over her mouth. "I am overwhelmed."

"You got any cookies?" He asked with a wide grin.

The Ornament

How the ornament came to me,
Is still very much a mystery.
It was a glorious Christmas day,
But I had to pushed it away.
The pain so tender and raw,
My own sorrow was all I saw.
People don't understand what soldiers do,
Nor what a soldier has to go through.
My little boy grew into a man,
The military was his decided plan.
He wanted to be like me, his dad,
Fight for our freedom as I had.
I said, 'wait son, this is a serious decision,'
But all he could see was me in his vision.
The night he left…a deep sad sigh,
All my wife and I did was cry.
I knew what was ahead for my son,
But he proudly put the uniform on.

Only a soldier's heart knows the true story,
What it takes to fly the Old Glory.
It isn't just what is demanded of you,
Nor the hell that each day you go through.
But the simple things you go without
What pains make your body shout
Sights that will forever fill your heart
Demons will haunt you way after you depart
The war isn't only bullets, tanks and guns
But the scars that steal the heart of our sons
Should he make it home alive…
He will fight a new battle to survive.
Questions of decisions made…
Scenes of lifeless bodies in your mind parade.
The wounds they receive to insure our peace,
Are scars of a soldier that will never cease.
The young men that join this sacred mission,
Will return broken and changed beyond recognition.

But this Christmas there will be no son,
We got the news of what had been done.
We looked again at the flag and plaque,
That was all that we had from the vicious attack.
That made our son a hero, but took his last breath,
He fought for our freedom to his very death.
We clung in tears to his pictures and letters once more,
We knew he would never again walk through our door.
My wife shivered in the coolness of the room
Was it the wintery season or the reality of gloom
I went out the door to get more wood
There was the ornament at my feet stood

I reached and picked it up as tears streamed
On top of a pair of soldiers boots it beamed
A ceramic ball in red, white and blue,
My son's dog tags hung on it too
we will never forget was etched in gold
My son's name and service dates were on the boots in bold
Forgetting the wood, I walked back inside
My tears and smile I could not hide.
My wife joined me in this sacred sight,
This mysterious gift that had been delivered by night.
This perfect ornament was a soothing balm
That healed the heart and made it calm
Someone had remembered…it was not in vain
Every tear had meaning not just pain
We placed the ornament in the center of the tree
The boots sit right under it for the free

We passed on the legacy of the mysterious ornament,
To another family whose son never made it home from
deployment.
We sat in the car with prayer and anticipation,
Knowing the emotions of losing a son for our nation.
When the door creaked open and the ornament revealed
Was all my wife and I needed to be fully healed
It is not in the taking that life grants peace
But in the giving that one receives full release
To every parent who puts their kid on freedom's alter,
Words of thanks, gratitude and appreciation falter.
Give respect, love and gratitude to the military around you,
Thank them for what they live without and what they do.

And should you find you like this story,
And someone you know died for Old Glory.
Pass along this mysterious ornament to those who grieve,
It will be quite the blessing to those who receive!

Peppermint Mocha

"Good morning, what can I get started for you?" The barista asked Lacey.

"Umm, let me get …" she looked in her wallet. "Umm…"

"Come on lady, make up your mind. Some of us have to work." The man behind her bellowed.

"Just give me the peppermint mocha."

"Coming right up." The barista said as he moved to fill her order.

"Oh, wait, can you make that with almond milk?" She dared to look over her shoulders. She could feel the man's dragon breath on her neck.

"Sure. You did say Grande right?"

Lacey switched her feet. "Oh, ummm, whatever is the biggest you got." She pulled out her day planner. Today was a full one. "Oh can you put three extra shots in that please." She tilted her head. "Been a rough morning."

"Lady, are you finally done? Just asking." The man behind her barked.

Lacey decided she would not respond to that. She had burnt the kids' breakfast and she was running late. If she wasn't careful, she would explode on this guy. She concentrated on what she needed to do first at work. She almost had her ducks in a row when the barista handed her a cup of liquid gold. She immediately took off the lid and sucked down the whipped cream.

Then she hurriedly turned to leave and ran smack into the man behind her. Her coffee cup slipped from her grasp and splashed all on him. "Oh my gosh! I am so so sorry." She grabbed some napkins. "It's all over your suit jacket, tie, and shirt." She said as she moved to wipe at it.

"Like that is going to help." He raised his hands. "Back away slowly. Don't touch me."

"Your poor wife," she said then popped hand over her mouth.

"Who says I have a wife?" He speared her with his angry eyes. "What a way to start the week." He growled through his clenched teeth and left.

"I am so sorry for this mess." She told the man behind the counter as she cleaned it up with another wad of napkins.

"Let me make you another drink." He smiled at her. "It's on the house."

"Oh dear, should I dare?" she put the napkins in the trash.

"Evidently you need one!" The barista said with a smile.

"Thank you so much," she said as she carefully reached for her new drink. "By the way, who was that guy? I feel really bad about *sharing* my coffee *all over* him. It was an accident. He was a jerk about it."

"He's a regular. I think he works at Rederick Innovations."

"Hmm, he was wearing a suit. What do you suppose he does there?"

"I don't know. But he comes in every morning and gets the same thing."

"Probably does accounts or advertising or something like that. Probably not the janitor."

"No I think not," The barista laughed. "But it might be advertising, he has more than once left one of the company's pens."

He showed her the pen. She twirled it in her hand. "Do you mind if I keep this?"

"Sure." He waved a hand. "Have a good one." He said and went on to help other customers.

She dropped the pen in her purse and mumbled, *I'm gonna try* and left.

"How was your day?" Lacey asked her oldest daughter Robin.

"It was great, mom!" she said as she shut the van door.

"That is good to hear. How did you do on that spelling test?"

Her daughter's disappearing smile answered that question.

"Guess what we did in art today? It was really cool."

"Robin, no changing the subject. I am sure what you did in art today was fantastic and that you were terrific at it. But what I want to know is how did you do on your spelling test."

She hung her head, "I got a D, mom."

Lacey exhaled, "Robin, you have to do better. When we get home and after dinner, bring me your speller and your test. We need to work on this."

"Would that be after we clean up, finish yesterday laundry, start some more and help Robert with his homework?"

Lacey glanced at her precious daughter. She knew the child was not being belligerent, but she was sending her mom a message. A tear slid out of her eye. She did not want Robin to see her crying so she decided to remain quiet and concentrate on her driving.

They picked up Reanna from daycare and went to Robert's soccer practice. Lacey sighed … *and after soccer practice.* The March wind ripped the words from her mouth as she played with Reanna. She pulled her thin sweater tighter. She just couldn't let her kids down.

Lord, I really could use some help right now. As she chased her sweet little one, she continued to pour her heart out to God.

"You did great, Robert. I'm so proud of you." Lacey messed her son's hair and gave him a proud momma wink.

"Oh mom, by the way, Coach said the uniforms are going to be $120.00 and I need to buy soccer cleats."

Her son babbled on, but she didn't hear him. How was she ever going to afford a uniform and cleats? She had to scrape up to pay the entry fee. It had been three years, right after Reanna was born that her husband had left them for another woman. He hadn't been very interested in the kids when he was there and hadn't contacted them since he left.

She told herself, *hold it together until you go to bed, Lacey, your pillow will be waiting to catch your tears.*

The next morning when she woke, she laughed. *I was too tired to cry, well if that doesn't beat all.*

As soon as her feet hit the floor, another day of the rat race started. Get dressed, get breakfast, make lunches, get the kids ready for school, rush them to the van, and try not to be late.

As they drove to school, Lacey quizzed Robin on her spelling words. "Have a great day you two!" She told them as she dropped Robin and Robert off at school.

"And now it's your turn my little stinkerdoodle." She smiled in her mirror as she looked at her sweet bundle of energy Reanna.

After she dropped Reanna off at the daycare, she was off to her job, only to retrace her steps seven hours later. If she wasn't careful, exhaustion would overwhelm her. She dug in her purse in search of some lipstick. *At least I can look decent,* she told herself. That's when she found his pen. She laughed, then sighed. *Another expense! I can't let him pay his dry-cleaning bill. I caused the accident, I should pay for it, but how?*

That is how she found herself at the coffee shop the next morning. She got there early. She didn't want to take a chance of running into *Mr. Unpleasant.*

"Can I help you," the same barista asked Lacey.

"Yes, do you remember me?"

"Yes ma'am. I don't forget a face."

"Well then, do you remember the man I covered in my coffee?"

He nodded.

"You mentioned he was a regular. So if you don't mind, could you give him this the next time he comes in?" She handed him an envelope.

"Sure." He looked at his watch. "He should be here in about 32 minutes."

"Thank you so much." Then she turned to leave.

"Are you not going to get a coffee ma'am?"

"Can't swing it today." She said and left. Then she stuck her head back in the door. "But have a great day!"

Three weeks passed and still Lacey noticed that the check she had written to *Mr. Unpleasant* had not cleared the bank. *Surely that barista didn't keep it?* She thought.

She decided to find out. She bit her nails as she rode up the elevator in the sky scrapper. She found the correct room number, which the woman at the counter had told her. With much trepidation, she opened the door.

"May I help you?" the secretary asked.

"Yes, I am here to see Mr. Un…I mean Umm." She saw him through the glass window. "Oh never mind, I got this."

As she went straight for his door, the secretary followed frantically behind her calling out. "You can't just barge in like that, he'll blow up."

Lacey went in anyway.

He swiveled around. "Excuse me?"

"I'm sorry sir, I tried to detain her," His secretary said.

He dismissed his secretary with a grunt.

"What brings you barging in here?" he asked looking at his watch.

She gulped, "Uh, well, uh did you get my card?"

"Yes I did."

"And…" she asked all the while wishing the floor would swallow her up.

"Look Ms? I don't even remember your name."

"Marllor, Lacey Marllor." She filled in for him.

"Whatever. I am the CEO of Rederick Innovations. I don't need your measly money. What I need is for you to get out of my office so I can work. You don't make it to the top by sitting on your tuft."

With her jaw on the floor she spoke, "Scrooge you! What you need is Jesus no doubt!" she turned and left.

Hot tears poured down her cheeks as she drove back to work. *Lord, how can one be so cruel? So uncaring?* On she prayed for this man. Then she stopped and repented of her ungodly reaction to him. Then she prayed some more. She washed her face and reapplied her make up and went in to finish her workday.

It was a soccer practice afternoon so when they left the field Robert asked his mom the question that had been plaguing her. "So mom, when are you going to pay the coach for my uniform?"

Lacey took a deep breath, "Robert, I have tried everything. But we have had some expenses come up and I'm … I'm not sure I can swing it, son." He was silent, but the look on his face crushed Lacey's heart.

She looked in the rearview mirror as she drove home. Robert's tear stained cheeks matched her own. Being a single parent had made Lacey do some strange things, and this was going to be outlandish. She made a quick decision and did a U-turn. She had one last trick up her sleeve. She just hoped the *magician* would play along. *Surely he is loaded …*

"Where are we going, momma?" Robin asked.

"You'll see." She said and winked at her daughter. Her thoughts were more like this … *a last ditch effort to get your brother a uniform and cleats.*

They pulled up to the sky scrapper and she told Robert to get out of the car. She knelt in front of him and spoke. "Listen to me, Robert, you are a fantastic soccer player," she messed his hair. She gave him the exact directions to *Mr. Unpleasant's* office. "Here is what I want you do. Go in and say, 'Excuse me sir, but I was wondering if you would be willing to sponsor me to play soccer. I have been practicing and I'm real good at it, but I need a uniform and cleats. It would be much appreciated.' Then give him the order information.

"Are you sure, mom?"

"No Robert, I'm not sure of anything anymore. But it's worth a try." He walked off. When he glanced back at her, she blew him a kiss and gave him an encouraging thumb up.

She got back in the car, "Okay, Robin, let's pray."

As soon as she saw him come back through the door with tears pouring down his cheeks, she knew the answer.

"Oh sweetie," she hugged him and he got in the car. "What did he say?"

He spoke between sniffles. "He told me to scram so I did. I took off out of there like my pants were on fire." He wiped his nose on the back of his hand. "How do you know this man anyway?"

"Don't worry about it, Robert. Right now what he needs is a big punch in the nose!" She said as she put the car in reverse.

"Just never mind, mom. It's okay. I'll try next year," Robert muttered.

"No Robert!" she hit the dash. "I will find a way." She said with her jaw set. "With the Lord, we will find a way." She said much more calmly.

Her poor pillow ...

Kingston leaned back in his chair, tapping his pen. He opened his desk drawer and took out the piece of torn paper. He rubbed his fingers across the name and address. Why had he kept this? He had been so uncaring when he tore up the check. Yet hours later, he reached into his trashcan and retrieved this. Why?

He did not know. But he did know this, as the pages of his life continued to turn, he was getting lonelier and lonelier. He had graduated college at the top of his class and he had built a company from the ground up. He had it all. He was rich, but he had no one to share it with. He wondered if this was all there is to life."

He called his secretary in. "Agnes," he stood and walked around. "Agnes, if you were going to, say, try to start dating, what, how I mean, what would you do?"

She cleared her throat and sat up straight. "I am married Mr. Rederick."

"Oh." His face flushed. "Did I know that?"

"I told you that information four years ago when you hired me."

"I see."

"However," she pushed up her black rimmed glasses. "If it were, say, someone like you, you might start by being around people." She started to stand. "Will that be all, Mr. Rederick?"

"Yes, Agnes."

She turned at the door, "And when you are around people, you might try being nice." She whispered and scooted out the door.

He raised his eyebrows at the closed door. He looked down at his desk. That is when he noticed the corner of the crumpled paper the boy had left. He grabbed it and flew out the door.

"Oh and Agnes." He went to her desk. "Call the coach of this team and purchase all the uniforms and cleats." He started to walk away. "Oh and bats, gloves, whatever equipment they need."

"Uh, sir, it's soccer." She cleared her throat. "They only use soccer balls."

"Yeah, I knew that." He walked toward his office. "Get whatever is needed." He went in his office. He stuck his head back out, "Thank you."

He walked around his office for hours. Then he left and went to a fancy restaurant to eat dinner. He had done this for years, but tonight, he seemed smothered by his aloneness.

"Mommy! Mommy!" Robert came running off the soccer field after practice.

"What? What is it, son?" Her heartbeat raced. She grabbed him and on her knees waited to hear what was wrong.

"Jesus did it! Jesus did it!" he shouted.

"What are you talking about?"

"He gave us all uniforms and cleats! And a whole bag of new balls!" He said and hugged his momma nearly knocking her over.

She couldn't help it; her pillow couldn't wait. The tears started. She eventually pulled back. "What great news! You know, Robert, I don't want you to think God is a magical genie. He didn't have to answer our prayers the way He did. I am as excited as you, but the lesson should be, even if He had chosen not to do this you would have still praised Him."

She went over to the coach to find out the name of this generous *Jesus* (benefactor). He said it had been an anonymous donor.

She smiled as she drove home. She thanked the Lord for His tender care. She had a special thank you plan forming.

A few days later, Lacey took the elevator at Rederick's Innovations to the top floor. She went through the door and this time stopped at Agnes' desk.

"How can I help you?" she asked.

"Please give Mr. Un... I mean, uh..."

"Mr. Rederick."

"Yes, Mr. Rederick, please give him this poster and this card."

"He is available if you would like to give it to him yourself." Agnes offered.

"Um, no, I think it will be fine for you to do it." She gave the poster to the secretary that held every team member's signature and individual words of thanks. She had also written a very kind note, team game schedule, along with a $10 coffee gift certificate.

She skipped out the door and went to work with joy. That weekend, Lacey started her morning in the kitchen trying to cook ahead for the coming week. She also did chores that didn't normally get done during the week. Not too long into morning, her three blessings woke up wanting breakfast.

They ate and readied for Robert's first game. Lacey got him all decked out in his uniform and cleats. "Okay, pose," Lacey said to Robert. Snap. Snap went her camera.

"Are you done yet mom?" He asked quickly getting tired of pictures and ready to go.

"Okay. Okay, I can't help doing the mommy thing." She messed his hair and loaded everyone up in the van.

The game started and Lacey was jumping up rooting for Robert who was on the field. She was startled when heard his voice.

"So which one is yours?" His deep voice boomed.

She turned to see, yes it was *Mr. Unpleasant*! She smiled and pointed. "He's over there. I know they kinda all look the same." Her thoughts were a whirl. *What in the world was this guy doing here?*

"He looks sharp in his uniform." Kingston boasted.

"They all do, Mr. Rederick." She gave him a much appreciative smile. "I can't thank you enough."

"Ah, it was nothing." He said with a contented grin.

"It may have been nothing to you, but it meant everything to my son. As a matter of fact, he thinks you're Jesus!" she chuckled.

"Whoa now. I've been called a lot of things, but not Jesus."

She thought, *Yes, and you would probably die if you knew what we called you!*

She cleared her throat. "As you have probably deduced, I'm a single mother of three precious children and we are on a tight budget. We could not afford his uniform and cleats. So we prayed for us to find a way. Though I scrimped and saved, I just couldn't swing it. So he had given up after his visit with you." She watched him processing her words.

"So why then did you send me a check for my dry-cleaning bill?" His eyebrows squished together almost making Lacey laugh.

"Mr. Rederick, we might be poor, but we have integrity. I damaged your clothes and restitution was the respectable thing to do."

He was silent a moment. "But you could have used that money for his uniform."

"No, the lesson was more important than the uniform." She checked on Reanna, who was playing in the dirt. "You don't always get your way in life. And integrity was more important than the money." She put a hand on his arm. "Money isn't everything."

He raised his eyebrows.

"And besides, then God couldn't show out like He did." She went back to watching the field. She went on to share how Robert had reacted the next practice when the donation was announced.

He snickered, "Yeah, me Jesus. That is laughable."

She heard him and laughed silently with him. *She figured why he came was to be a proud peacock about his donation, but why was he staying?*

He watched the entire game. Robert's team won and he came running to his momma yelling his victories.

She swooped him up in a giant hug and congratulations and set him back on his feet.

"You did real good, son," Kingston said as he patted him on the back.

Robert looked at his mom.

"Robert, this is your *Jesus*, Mr. Rederick."

"Really, you were the one Jesus told to buy us uniforms?" He barreled a hug right into his legs.

He chuckled. "Something like that, kid."

She introduced Robin and Reanna to him. "Girls, this is *Mr. Un...* I mean Mr. Rederick."

He shook Robin's hand and tapped Reanna on the nose who was nestled on Lacey's hip.

"Hey how about celebrating. We could get pizza or whatever?"

"We would love to, but like I mentioned, eating out is not in our budget right now."

"It's on me," he said.

"Well now don't you think that would be awkward?" She put it out there for what it was.

He rubbed the back of his neck. "Hmm. Not to me. Would it help if I begged?" She saw a twinkle in his eye and actually felt he was sincere.

"Okay, Mr. Rederick, we will join you so long as you know we are poor but not starving."

They went to a pizza parlor and Lacey actually found she was having a good time. As she stole glances at *Mr. Unpleasant* she thought his smile sure meant he was, too.

"So, did my mom tell you what we nick named you?" Robin asked Kingston.

He looked at Lacey with raised eyebrows, "Why no she didn't. Do tell."

"Robin!" Her mother said through clenched teeth.

Suddenly and without preamble, Robert answered, "*Mr. Unpleasant.*" He was unaware of the stares as he shoved another piece of pepperoni in his mouth.

Then Kingston roared in laughter, everyone followed suit. "WOW! *Mr. Unpleasant* and Jesus all in one day. Shew!" He shook his head. It lightened the mood around the table.

He leaned over for Lacey's ears only, "I don't do people very well."

She leaned and whispered back, "I don't do coffee very well."

He cracked a big grin and said. "I can help with that if you will help me with the other."

"That's a deal, Mr. Rederick!" she licked her fingers before shaking his hand.

Lacey noticed Kingston showed up to every game that summer. If a game fell on a Saturday, he ended up somehow spending the day with them. She was not sure how this happened, but what really scared her was *that she liked it.*

That evening, Kingston kicked back in his recliner and grabbed the remote. He flipped through the channels and ended up turning the TV off. *I couldn't be falling for her?* He laughed at his own joke. The thought wouldn't leave him.

He was glad that he had met this woman and her kids, for no other reason than to re-direct his life back to Jesus. He had been doing his own thing for 15 years and he was reminded through a little boy's childlike faith the importance of a relationship with the Almighty God. He had repented of the worship of money and self-idolatry.

He reminisced over the summer months. He had changed a lot, he knew, but was what he felt *love*? The thought of an instant family scared him out of his wits. How does one date with three attachments?

Summer turned into fall and with Lacey's favorite time of year just around the corner, she seemed to have an extra measure of joy. She felt a sting of sadness when Robert had his last game. For that had been their connection and she wondered what would happen to *Mr. Unpleasant* ... no she couldn't call him that anymore, Mr. Pleasant.

"Well, what a season. Robert, you did really well. I'm proud of you." Kingston said and actually found himself hugging the boy.

"Well, so I guess this is it, huh?" she said as she rocked on her heals.

He raised his eyebrows and cracked a grin. "Yes, I think so, that is unless you will agree to call me Kingston. This whole Mr thing makes me feel old."

"Okay, Kingston, where from here?" she searched his eyes. She didn't even know what she felt for this man much less was she even ready for a commitment again, if ever.

"I don't know. You're asking a man who just started doing people." He touched her shoulder and stared straight in her eyes. "And this beautiful blonde and her kids keep distracting me something crazy."

She smiled. "We are going to the pumpkin patch next Saturday; why don't you join us?"

"Okay I will." He walked her and the kids to the van "What have I just signed myself up for?"

She laughed, "A lot of fun! I hope so anyway."

The next Saturday at the pumpkin patch, they had a sunflower seed contest, potato sack race and took turns using the gigantic pumpkin trebuchet. Afterward, they took the hay wagon down to the patch area. They were casually walking looking at the pumpkins. The kids were weaving in and out of the patch laughing. Kingston's hand hit Lacey's and latched on to her pinky finger.

A sense of warmth traveled through her. The longing to be held again was strong. She closed her eyes at the onslaught of emotion, but she still did not let go of the tiniest hope.

Reanna came wobbling out, "Momma, can we get this one?"

Kingston swooped her up, "You are so adorable. Do you know that?" He said and tapped her on the nose. "Of course you can have it."

"Excuse me?" Lacey cleared her throat. "Kingston?"

"What?"

"Can I talk to you in private?" They walked a few feet away from where the kids were playing. "We cannot afford a pumpkin that size for one. Kingston, you aren't our *sugar daddy*. You don't have to buy our affection. You already have it."

He let out a low whistle and rubbed the back of his neck. "I just want to give her the moon, so what's a little pumpkin?"

Lacey laughed. "For one, that ain't no little pumpkin. Two, you evidently have not been around kids much. It nearly takes the moon to raise them."

"I have money, Lacey, and it's no trouble." He pleaded his case.

"Yes, but you already paid for our tickets in here. Plus, you already bought us all roasted corn cobs. I have worked really hard at managing our money and teaching the kids that they can't always get what they want."

He looked into her eyes. "I don't understand, but I will abide by your wishes. Can they all get at least a *small* pumpkin? On me?"

She sighed, "I guess, a very *small* pumpkin."

They went back to the kids and he told them they could all get a little pumpkin. They shouted their joy and went to find their treasures. On the way to the hay bale maze, he stopped and got them both a pumpkin Latte.

"Ohh, now you are definitely making points," she said as she closed her eyes and enjoyed her first sip of the welcoming warm liquid. She opened her eyes only to find him staring at her. "Thank you."

He brushed her check with the back of his hand. "No, I am the one who needs to thank you."

"For what?"

"So many things." They began to walk. "I guess the biggest is how I allowed money to govern my life instead of God. And that life can be full of joy without much money. It's all about giving." He took a sip of his coffee. "Those, my sweet lady, are some big lessons."

She often found him holding her hand or his arm around her shoulders. That night her pillow, once again held her tears, but this time they were tears of joy.

December was in full swing. At his request, Lacey had given Kingston a schedule of their events for the month. He planned to attend everything he could.

Lacey had to admit it was awkward to have him sit with her and put his arm behind her during the kids' Christmas play. She supposed if anything came of this, there would be gossip soon enough.

It was the Saturday before Christmas and they were going caroling that night. They baked cookies all day. Kingston and Lacey had as much fun as the kids.

"I really had no ideas what all went into baking cookies, much less this many. What a kind heart you have, Lacey." Kingston told her as she rolled out more sugar cookie dough.

"Kingston, this is my absolute favorite time of year. People seem to be a bit more open to hear the story of baby Jesus who came to set us free. Folks are more kind and accepting of kindnesses given."

Kingston raised his eyebrows. "I know the meaning of Christmas. But something tells me, as it has already begun, there is a whole lot more to Christmas that I have been missing."

"Christmas is all about others. Jesus came not for Himself but for others. So we in turn should try to be like Him."

He let out a low whistle. "You got an awesome mom right there," he told the kids. They chorused their love back.

That night they bundled up against the bitter cold air. They went house to house singing Christmas carols and giving a package of cookies to each household. They were on their fifth house, in the middle of *Silent Night*, when these words reached Lacey's ears ...

"I love you."

She knew the voice. She felt his breath on her neck as he huddled behind her singing. She froze ... and not because of the falling temperatures, for she was suddenly flushed head to toe, but froze stiff.

When she didn't move, he asked, "Did you hear me?"

She ever so slightly nodded.

"Are you okay?" His voice wavered.

She knew he was concerned, but this wasn't the place. She put aside that the man she had fallen in love with had just confessed his love to her. This was no easy feat, but on they went giving the love of Jesus out in a cookie and a song.

That night when Lacey walked him to the door she softly spoke. "Love is a scary word to me. I have had my heart broken." A tear slipped out.

He wiped it with his thumb. "Then he never really had your heart." He dug in his pocket. "This is an early Christmas present."

"Oh, Kingston, you didn't need to do this."

"Oh yes I did. It looks to me like you might just need a year supply."

She had it open by then. It was a gift certificate to the coffee shop where they had first met.

She covered her mouth at the remembrance. She put her hand on his arm, "Thank you."

Exactly three days before Christmas, Lacey decided she needed to use her certificate. The long nights and extra activities were catching up to her. She walked in barely awake and ordered her peppermint mocha with four extra shots. She rubbed her shoulders and stretched her neck willing her body to get with the game. It was morning, but her body was not agreeing with the clock.

The barista handed her a peppermint mocha.

"Thank you and Merry Christmas!"

He returned the sentiment but she did not hear it. She had turned in her haze and hurry and collided smack into someone ... spilling her mocha all over the front of ...

"King ..." But she was cut off by his lips sealing hers in the most wonderful kiss ever. Fulfilling every longing that she had.

When he released her, her head was spinning. "What was that for?"

He had the biggest smile as he took of his now coffee drenched tie. "Well God and I have been having a lot of talks. And I asked Him for a sign. Honey, you can't get a bigger sign that this." He pointed to his clothes.

She shook her head confused. "A sign for what? A klutz? Time to find a new coffee shop?"

He tried hard not to laugh. He put both hands on her face. "For this. Will you marry me?"

Tears began to stream and she pulled back. "I'm not sure you know what you're getting into." She paused. "I'm scared."

"You're right I have no idea what I'm doing, but I want us to do it together. And I'm scared out of my wits."

"I need some time," she said.

"I have all the time in the world. While you're waiting, will you wear this?" He put a box in her hands, gave her a quick kiss, and left the coffee shop.

"Now that was a completely different ending than before," the barista said with a smile.

The Candy Cane

"Ahhh. It must have been the first day with the kids," Nathaniel said as he walked into the kitchen.

"How can you tell?" Betsy bantered as she stood in front of a counter covered with apples.

Nathaniel wrapped his arms around his wife and whispered in her ear, "I love you. I hope you had a great first day. They are a blessed class to have you for their teacher."

She turned to face her husband of seven years and straightened his tie as she spoke. "You were probably every teacher's dream student." She kissed him, "And I love you to the moon and back!"

Betsy turned and looked at all the apples. The tradition of giving the teacher an apple on the first day of school was still in full force at Harbow Elementary.

"I think it's amazing that no two apples are the same, just like no two students are the same," she said as she picked up one. "I have a feeling this one will have me in tears."

He took the apple out of her hand to look at it more closely.

"Let me guess. She is a quiet, sweet little girl, who has little means, but already loves her teacher."

"Yep, and these," she picked up two other apples, "are two bullies who made fun of her apple when she gave it to me."

"That just rips your heart out."

"It does for sure. However, I'm there to love on these kids, both the *ripe* and the *rotten* apples."

"Good morning class," Betsy said as she rang her bell. Everyone quieted and she took roll call. When she got to Mercy Ann, she slipped up her hand to indicate her presence. She gave Betsy a sweet smile. *In just three weeks that girl has made roots in my heart!* Betsy thought to herself.

Betsy glared at the two boys snickering at Mercy Ann. Betsy stood up, "I will not tolerate bullying in my class." She stared at the two boys until they looked away.

"Now, as you know, last week I gave the class an assignment in which we would learn a few aspects of writing and speaking. Even though you are only fourth graders, it's a good start that you will build on each coming year." She pointed to the board. "On the board I have divided the class into assigned days. The first group to share starts today."

She had put Mercy Ann in the first group, second person to share. "So, students, remember, your topic is: What or who I want to be when I grow up. You have to give three reasons why and three ways you plan to achieve this goal. Stand straight and speak loud and clear. Okay, Brandon, I believe you are first."

After Brandon finished the teacher called for the next student. "Mercy Ann, you are next."

She watched the little girl slip from her seat. Betsy noted that this was the third time she had worn that dress since the beginning of school. It was always clean and pressed. Her long hair was unimpressive but always brushed. She nodded for Mercy Ann to start.

Mercy Ann had taken a hand-sewn bag to the front of the class with her. She reached in and pulled out a seed packet. "When I grow up, I want to be like my mom." She showed the seed pack. "My mom makes things grow from seeds and she's real good at it. She grows all kinds of food for us to eat." Then she pulled out a spatula. "This represents all the yummy things my mommy cooks. She makes the best cakes, pies, and oh the cookies. I want to grow up to make people smile with a spatula. And third reason is this," she reached in her bag and pulled out a needle and thread. "If I could sew half as good as my momma, I would be proud. She makes all our clothes."

There were some snickers and jabs in the room, but Mercy Ann wasn't finished. "Three easy ways to accomplish this goal are 1) Watch my momma and read books, 2) Copycat right beside her, and 3) Pray asking Jesus to help me." She did a curtsy and sat back down.

"Thank you, Mercy Ann. I am sure if your mom had heard you she would be honored." She called the other three students one at a time, then they went onto another subject.

When lunchtime came, Betsy knew where she needed to be ... sitting with Mercy Ann. Sadly, she knew other children would make fun of the child, so when Betsy saw her sitting down, she got her lunch and sat across from her. "Do you mind if I sit here, Mercy Ann?"

"No, ma'am." She replied with a smile.

Betsy had to swallow past the lump in her throat as she saw what Mercy Ann was eating. It wasn't gross; it just wasn't much. She had a piece of homemade bread folded over with peanut butter inside. She had some cucumber slices and a small gnarly apple.

Betsy felt a twinge of guilt as she had an overflowing hot plate. She cleared her throat, "Mercy Ann, you did a great job in class today."

"Thank you, Mrs. Lawrence. I was nervous. But I prayed and Jesus helped me."

Mercy Ann finished her meal and wiped her mouth on her cloth napkin, put everything back in her paper sack and folded it neatly, Betsy assumed for re-use. Then she spoke, "Mrs. Lawrence, will you excuse me for a moment?"

"Sure." She watched Mercy Ann walk to the water fountain and take a long drink. Betsy thought she was not going to live through the day much less the year. In no time, Mercy Ann gracefully sat back across from her teacher.

Since no one ever sat with Mercy Ann, Betsy felt free to question her. "Tell me about your parents and brothers and sisters."

Mercy Ann's eyes flickered. "Um okay. Really, there isn't much to tell. I have a wonderful mom and a hard working dad. I don't have brothers or sisters."

"I see. Do you get lonely for someone to play with?"

Mercy Ann shrugged. "No, not really. I help my mom a lot in the garden and in the kitchen. I help her hang out the laundry. I don't know. I just sorta stay busy. If I have time, I might sit at the table and color or draw. In the winter, I read by the fire. But mom promises to teach me to quilt this winter."

"Wow, you have a busy life."

"When my dad comes home, I go with him to do the chores on the farm. He used to carry me on his back and bounce me around. Now I'm too big, so he pulls my pigtails and calls me Little Sprout. Though he's a big man, the biggest part of him is his heart."

She looked away. "I know I'm different and that people make fun of me." Then she looked back at Betsy. Tears had bubbled in her eyes but had not yet spilled over. "Mrs. Lawrence, what they don't understand is that I feel sorry for them. Because in my *nothing* I have *everything*."

Betsy raised her eyebrows. *Wow! That's a huge truth.* She thought. "Mercy Ann, you seem wise beyond your years. Don't hesitate to tell me if anything ever gets out of hand with other students."

It was time for her to get back to class, so she left her precious lunch partner and went back to her classroom.

After that, a few times a week there would be something fresh on her desk. She knew who left it there. She would leave a sticky note of thanks on her desk. She loved to see Mercy Ann smile.

"Let me guess, purple hull peas with cornbread for dinner?" Nathaniel asked his wife when he came home from work and saw her shelling them. "More garden blessings from Mercy Ann?"

"Uh huh," she laughed. "I guess my fingers will match hers tomorrow."

"What do you mean?"

"Bless her heart, she had purple fingers." She shook her head. "When I asked her about it she slid them under her legs and told me why."

"And?"

She pointed at her pan. "Shelling these little buggers. Though I'm sure she did it for hours on end. I am only doing it for a meal."

She was quiet as she finished and put some water in the pot to cook them. She let out a big sigh. "It is so hard for me to see children make fun of her. Why do kids have to be so mean?"

"I don't know, sweetie, but it just carries on through their life. I work in a white-collar working class and we have jerks there too. You have to remember a lot of times those mean kids are the ones who need the most attention and have the worst home life."

"That's it. I remember Mercy Ann said something profound to me that first day I ate lunch with her."

Nathaniel raised his eyebrow. "And ...?"

"She said that she felt sorry for the kids that make fun of her because in her nothing she had everything."

"Yeah, that's pretty profound alright. She's right though."

"I'll admit she's probably the most peculiar student I have ever had. I have only been teaching five years, but that is remarkable."

Nathaniel put his hand on her shoulder and squeezed. "I know you are in this profession to make a difference. But perhaps this time, God has it for Mercy Ann to make a difference in you."

With that in mind, Betsy set out to see what she could

learn. She began to watch Mercy Ann in earnest. What she saw was eye opening. Every morning the child greeted the decrepit, ancient janitor. She spoke kind words to him if he was ever cleaning anywhere around her. Betsy didn't think she had ever given the old man a thought.

On more than one occasion as the class passed the janitor going to gym or lunch they would say unkind things to him or knock his mop down. She actually spoke up for him. Then she would get out of line to go pick up his mop. She gave him a little wave every time she passed him. Betsy also saw that a few times each week she gave him something. He would pat her on the head and put it in his pocket.

Mercy Ann stopped by Betsy's desk one morning before the other students arrived. "Good morning Mercy Ann, did you need something?"

She put her index finger to her lips and signaled for the teacher to follow her. They tiptoed down the hall into another wing then she pointed. "What is he doing?" she whispered in her teacher's ear.

Betsy tilted her head, then had to get control of her emotions. "That is a dear old man praying for each student." They both watched again and then tiptoed back to their classroom.

Betsy excused herself and she went to her car and burst into tears. *"Lord ... if you show me anymore, I'm not sure I can handle it."* She prayed. She tried to fix her make up before heading back to class to start the day.

October came in a hurry. With it was pumpkin pie and apple cider. Leaves were falling making a beautiful blanket on the earth's floor. Betsy noticed Mercy Ann still wore the same three dresses only with a threadbare sweater over them. Betsy assumed she only had one pair of shoes.

"What is that wonderful smell coming from the oven?" Nathaniel asked his wife.

"It, my lovely husband, is fresh pumpkin pie."

"Really?" He asked and tapped her on the nose. "Come sit with me."

He sat in his burgundy wing back chair and patted his leg for her to sit in his lap. She easily obliged.

"So my sweet luscious pumpkin pie maker, how are you? And what has God been teaching you in class?"

"Oh my goodness, I don't know where to begin." She fully relaxed in his arms while she shared. She was nearly asleep when the beeper went off. "Don't want to burn my first pumpkin pie!" she jumped up and ran to the stove.

Over dessert, Betsy shared yet another amazing story. "Apparently this morning out on the school grounds as Mercy Ann was coming to class, her arms loaded with books, she was *bumped* into by a *rotten apple*. Of course, there was an immediate crowd, which followed suit in laughing at her. She was sobbing by the time she got to her desk. I took her out in the hall, wiped her tears, and hugged her."

"Wow!" Nathaniel said. "Just makes you want to make some applesauce out of some of those rotten apples, doesn't it?"

"Yeah. I have to really hold myself in check."

"How did you find out?" Her husband asked, getting seconds. "By the way … this is the best pumpkin pie I think I have ever had!"

"Another student in class told me. Just breaks my heart." She wagged her finger at him "Are you even gonna eat your dinner?"

"Hmmm … I thought this was dinner!" He winked at her.

"Last week, she actually brought the janitor a pie. From what I have observed, that child would go without in order to give to others. Where does someone learn such generosity? It shamed me."

"It has to be her upbringing. She has probably watched her parents do the same. Love does amazing things, way beyond what the heart can imagine."

"She has taught me so much already. I was thinking of inviting her to the Fall Festival at church. What do you think?"

"I think that's a great idea, but I know you have to be careful to follow the rules. I would love to meet the little cherubim myself."

As it turned out, Betsy got her wish to meet Mercy Ann's parents in the most unusual way. Not the way she would have ever thought. Betsy wrung her hands as she waited on the parents to arrive in the principal's office.

Not long after the door opened, the biggest man Betsy had ever seen walked in with a tiny woman following him. Betsy watched Mercy Ann burst into tears and run into the hefty arms of her father.

He squatted down and wiped her tears away. "Are you okay, Little Sprout?"

Mercy Ann nodded. Then her father stood.

Betsy put out her hand, "Hi Mr. and Mrs. Stevens. Thank you for coming. Betsy shook hands with both parents.

"What's this about, Mrs. Lawrence?" Danny Stevens asked.

Betsy cleared her throat. "Mercy Ann was involved in an altercation and has been given three days of afterschool detention."

She heard Mrs. Stevens gasp and watched her put her hand to her throat.

"What happened?" Mr. Stevens' calm question surprised Betsy. Mercy Ann still clung to her daddy's legs.

"First of all, I want you to know you have a precious daughter. This afternoon, the kids were coming back from lunch when a group of naughty boys agitated our janitor and dumped over his mop bucket. They were very rude and cruel to the old man. Before any teacher could get to the situation, your daughter stood in the gap and took up for the janitor telling the boys to quit being hateful. Well as things sometimes do, it escalated from there. Then she became the focal point and the boy pushed her down in the mop water."

There was a long silence. "Are you finished? I was waiting to hear what my daughter did wrong."

Betsy rubbed her hands together. "The rule here at Harbow Elementary states that anyone involved in an altercation, whether retaliation is administered, both students are disciplined."

Danny Stevens pulled his daughter from his legs and spoke directly to her. "Little Sprout, is what Mrs. Lawrence said true?"

Mercy Ann nodded yes and buried her head back in her dad's legs.

"And were the boys who were unreasonably rude to the janitor punished?"

"Sadly no."

"Why is there such discrepancy?" Mr. Stevens asked.

The principal spoke up at this point. "Mr. Stevens, if the janitor does not file a complaint, our hands are tied."

Both parents had thoughtful expressions.

Mr. Stevens pulled his daughter back so he could see her face and spoke. "Little Sprout, rules are rules. Though your intentions were good, in defending the janitor you landed yourself in a situation beyond your control. You take your punishment. But know in your heart you did a very noble thing." Then he looked at the adults and said, "May we all learn from the man with the mop and bucket."

He kissed his daughter on the forehead. Then he shook the principal's and Betsy's hand and bid them farewell.

His wife followed suit duplicating her husband's actions.

Betsy let out a big sigh. "Okay Mercy Ann, let's get back to class."

"Mrs. Lawrence, why is everyone so mean to Mr. James?" Mercy Ann asked Betsy as they walked back to class.

"That's hard to answer. But probably because he has a limp and is missing part of his left arm."

"What does that have to do with anything?"

"It shouldn't, but kids and adults alike think just because someone is different they are weird or somehow lesser of a person."

"If they got to know Mr. James, they would like him. He's very kind. I hate it when other kids laugh at him when he's cleaning the bathrooms. They make messes just to watch him clean them up. It has to be hard for him."

"I would imagine so." Betsy said as they entered the class and their conversation dropped.

Betsy waited for a week before inviting Mercy Ann and her family to the church festival.

The night of the festival, Nathaniel and Betsy worked the ring toss booth. It had been in full swing for an hour when Betsy saw them. She jabbed her husband. "There she is! She came!"

"Where?" her husband began scanning the room. Then he followed his wife's finger to who he thought was probably Mercy Ann. A big smile spread across his face.

"I'm going over and say hi. You got this?" she asked.

"Got it!" he said and watched her nearly run across the room. He watched her hug the little girl then shake hands with her parents. He was sure she was giving them the best welcome ever.

Soon his wife came bounding back. "Isn't she a cutie pie?"

"Yep, all 5 feet and 6 inches!" he said with a grin.

"Not me," she said as she gave him a love tap on the arm. "Mercy Ann."

"Yes, she is adorable. Can't wait for her to stop by here."

Betsy found it hard to concentrate and not look around at

her invited guests, but she did her best. She was having fun with all the kids, and watching her husband interact with the kids made all the set up and tear down worth it.

"Hi again, Mr. and Mrs. Stevens and Mercy Ann. Are ya'll having a good time?" Betsy asked as her student and parents entered their booth.

"Yes we are. It was kind of you to invite us. Thank you." Mr. Stevens said.

"Mercy Ann talks very highly of you. We are blessed that she has such a wonderful teacher this year." Mrs. Stevens told Betsy.

"Thank you. Believe me, I would love to have a classroom full of Mercy Anns." She motioned for her husband. "I would like to introduce you to my husband." She did the introductions then Nathaniel took over.

"It is so nice to finally meet the two of you, Mr. and Mrs. Stevens. And this is the cherubim I have heard so much about." He had squatted down to Mercy Ann's level. "Glad to meet you." He picked up her hand and kissed it.

"Would you like to play ring toss? I'm sure you'll be a winner!" Nathaniel said. They played several rounds before moving on. Nathaniel put his arm around his wife. "They are exactly like you told me. What a sweet family."

Betsy was having lunch again with Mercy Ann. "So how was your Thanksgiving?"

"Oh, Mrs. Lawrence, it was the best!" Her face lit up as she answered.

"Really? Why is that?"

"We invited Mr. James and he came!"

"That was kind. I bet that made Mr. James feel special."

"I think so. He told us he was wounded in the war. He talked a lot about his wife who passed away over 20 years ago. He talked about God and how important it was to follow Him."

"Wow, sounds like you really got to know him."

"Yes, ma'am. He's so quiet and humble. But when you get to know him you find out he's also full of kindness and wisdom."

"Seems there is a lot more to that man than a mop and a bucket."

"Oh yes, a whole lot more."

"Did your momma fix turkey and all the trimmings?"

"No, ma'am. We couldn't buy a turkey this year, but we fixed two of our yard birds. Momma makes the best roasted, stuffed chicken. We had other things from our garden like peas and corn. Of course stuffed eggs and cornbread dressing. Mom made homemade rolls and fresh honey butter."

"Sounds like a feast."

"It was." Mercy Ann licked her lips.

"And you probably had pie right?"

"You know it. Mom made pecan, pumpkin, and apple pies."

"Ummm. You're making my mouth water."

"We sent a big pan full of left overs and a pie home with Mr. James." Mercy Ann crinkled up her face. "He cried."

"He was probably so touched by your family's kindness."

"I gave him a big hug before he left."

"I bet that he had the best Thanksgiving ever."

"I don't know about him, but we sure did."

"It's time to get back to class, but I wanted to tell you how proud I am of you. Your efforts in math are paying off. Your test scores are improving. And here we are on the edge of December."

"I am trying. It helps to know I can come to you and ask you to explain a concept until I get it."

"That is what makes a teacher a teacher." She patted her hand and took up her tray.

On the first day of December, Betsy watched as Mercy Ann slid into her desk. Her eyes lighted as she picked up the candy cane and twirled it in her hand. She had gotten one each day of December last year in third grade.

She looked at all the other desks. Each one sported a candy cane too. "Thank you Mrs. Lawrence."

"For what sweetie?"

"For the candy canes."

Betsy raised her eyebrows. "I didn't do that. They were already here when I got here this morning."

Mercy Ann tilted her head. "Who did then?"

"Hmmm, I honestly don't know who our candy cane benefactor is!" She raised the one on her desk. "But whoever it is has been doing it all the years I have been here. He or she has never missed a desk or a day in December."

"That is strange. Not even the principal knows?"

"No. I think this has been going on for many years before I came. And still no one has ever solved The Candy Cane Caper mystery!"

"Whoever it is … picked my favorite."

Their conversation ended as kids filled up the class and the crinkle of cellophane paper filled the room.

The next day Mercy Ann found the janitor, "Good morning, Mr. James. Momma sent some Christmas cookies for you." She handed him a baggie of her momma's first batch of Christmas cookies.

"Sweet child, you put Christmas in my day. Give your parents my greetings." He took the proffered cookies and patted Mercy Ann on the head. Then she bounded off to class.

"Again!" she went straight to her desk … another candy cane lay on it. And the same for the rest of the week.

Monday of the next week, she brought her momma's second batch of Christmas cookies. Mercy Ann loved the way the janitor's grey eyes nearly turned blue when she spoke to him.

Every day that week in every classroom of every grade, there was a candy cane on each desk. Each morning, Mercy Ann would twirl her candy cane and stretch her mind and detective skills to solve *who* the mysterious Candy Cane Caper was.

On Wednesday of the following week, Mercy Ann got her biggest clue. She walked into class that morning … not a single candy cane anywhere! Zilch! None in her class. So she ran and peeked in the other class rooms and not a single candy cane anywhere.

She sat tapping her pencil. "Is everything alright Mercy Ann?" Betsy asked.

"I'm just thinking about our Candy Cane Caper. Isn't it so strange that all of the sudden, there aren't any?"

"Yes, it is. I was pretty shocked myself this morning." She sighed. "Very strange indeed." Before they could finish conversing, the class filled up with yapping kids looking under desks for missing candy canes.

Finally, Betsy called the class to attention. "Let's be quiet please for roll call." She cleared her throat and spoke. "Before I begin, I know this really throws you off. If you or your siblings have been here at Harbow for the past five plus years, you are wondering why on this day there are no candy canes. I don't know. But I want to make this a teaching moment." She had a dazed bunch of eyes looking at her. "We have gotten so used to the gift of the candy cane that we forgot the giver. We have become complacent and assume that the giver somehow owes us a candy cane." She stemmed her tears. "The person who gives out the candy canes owes us nothing. Let's be appreciative of what has been given not what was withheld." Then she proceeded with roll call. It was a very sobering day.

The next morning Mercy Ann skipped into class. "Good morning, Mrs. Lawrence." She said and gave her a hug. She had been doing that ever since the church festival. She looked at her desk and let out a sigh. "No canes again." Then she turned to her teacher. "Mrs. Lawrence, I was looking for Mr. James. Momma made him her last batch of cookies, my favorite, but I didn't see him in his usual place."

"Hmm. No, but I tell you what. I will check at lunch if he came to work today and let you know. How about that?"

"Oh yes, thank you very much."

Betsy thought she had just handed her the moon.

At lunch, she found Mercy Ann sitting in her usual seat, by herself. She sat down across from her. "I did what I promised, and then snooped around a little further. It happens to be that our precious Joseph James took a spill over the weekend and broke his leg. He is at Columbia Medical."

Mercy Ann put her hand over her mouth and gasped. There was a moment of silence then Betsy saw Mercy Ann's eyes sparkle and get huge. "He's The Candy Cane Caper!!" she said.

Betsy tilted her head and processed this information and then her eyes twinkled. "I think you are right!" she sighed, "Oh my goodness, after all these years! We finally figured it out. Oh my goodness."

"He is The Candy Cane Caper." Mercy Ann repeated herself. "Wow that is a lot of candy canes. That would be a lot of money."

Both were silent. Then Betsy went out on a limb and spoke. "Normally these kinds of things are taboo, but I was just wondering would you like to go with me to visit him? I will of course get permission from your parents first."

"Oh yes." She said and clapped her hands.

Betsy picked Mercy Ann up that evening. She had worn her best dress. Her mom waved from the porch as they drove off.

Mercy Ann grabbed Betsy's hand as they exited the elevator. She had never been in a hospital before. They tapped on James's door and then went in.

His mouth dropped open when he saw his visitors. "Hi, Mr. James, we have been missing you at school." Betsy said.

Mercy Ann reached up and as best as she could and hugged his neck. Then without any needed words, she pulled something out of her hand-sewn bag and laid it on the janitor's table.

Tears began to stream down Mr. James's cheeks. For a heart made from joining two candy canes together lay in front of him.

"You figured it out," he said in a feeble voice.

"All these years, Mr. James, how did you do it?" Betsy asked.

He pointed to heaven. "All kinds of miracles happen in December." He wiped a tear. "The best of them all ... *Joy to the World!*

Christmas Scraps

Tidbits from my heart to yours

The Paperclip Christmas

Christmas, 2017

My job in decorating the tree has always been to put the hanger hooks on the ornaments while others hang them on the tree. Now some 33 years later, the "others" are back to just my husband and me. Our 3 sons are all on their own. Nostalgia overcomes me as I open each box (some looking quite weathered).

Our first tree sparkled gold. My in-laws had giving us all their gold balls as they moved on to a new theme, so it was gold garland, gold beads, and gold balls (lots of them!). We had two very special ornaments. One was of glass and stated *Our First Christmas Together*. The other was an oval locket ornament that stated the same but inside we put our picture. Sigh. Looking at those pictures now, I realize how time has flown.

Not a single gold ornament remains. Over the years, we replaced them with "special" ornaments, like the glove ornament my sister gave me the year she insisted on an ornament exchange. Now as I place it on the tree, I think of her. It used to be just an ornament, but now it's a cherished memory.

As I open some boxes, my heart sinks. I remember the year our tree fell over twice. We lost several dated ornaments that year. We also lost the ornament I had kept since 6th grade (I'm 50 now). It was just a red ball with my name done in glitter, but my teacher had given it to me. I kept as many of the broken balls that I could; they remain in their torn boxes each year. It's a reminder that these are just *things*.

As I travel through the dated ornament years (including the broken ones), tears threaten. Each one is symbolic of our life at the time. One pitiful *plastic* ball has about lost its top, but it tells of a really hard year. So I put it up every year (it won't break!), and with it is a reminder of those less fortunate, and a challenge not to forget them.

Now I reach in and get baby's first Christmas ornaments. We have three sons, and doting grandparents gave ornaments too, so our tree blossomed quickly with the addition of each precious child. These ornaments try to bring wetness to my cheeks. The baby pictures, the baby balls, each bring strong memories. The baby book and shoe all hang in my heart and on the tree. Ahhh, such a tender moment.

I hang a few musical ornaments and laugh as I push their buttons, their songs long gone, but still the memories linger.

Then I unwrap the *ugly* ornaments. You know, the ones you find a *great place* for on the BACK of the tree. The ceramic churches, hands, and such, covered with every color offered by two and three year olds! This year, I proudly put them on the FRONT of the tree for they mean love!

There are those ornaments given to us by special friends. Their faces swim through my heart as I reach for their ornament. I smile as I hang the shell ornaments we collected (some are broken – don't look at their back side!) while living on the coast of California.

Oh and the travel ornaments, how can I forget those! The year we took a cruise with friends. The trip to D.C., Hawaii, and New York. We even have Mickey Mouse up there. My husband brought an ornament from Russia when he was on a business trip. He also spent six months in Kuwait, so that is the ornament for this year. Not that I really want to remember the separation, but the sacrifice he made for his family.

I didn't realize just how much of *life* our Christmas tree held on its branches!

As I hang each ornament, there is a clear reminder of harder times. The old, ill-formed paperclips that I attached to so many ornaments remind me of the years we couldn't afford the luxury of *real* hangers. I started to replace them, but then I decided to keep them as a reminder of God's provision even in the lean years.

I strung cranberries and popcorn for the traditional tree garland all alone this year. Yet with every popcorn piece and every cranberry, I have much to be thankful for, so, we don't have a fancy themed tree like some.

Nor do we have exquisite decorations, but we have a *Paperclip Tree of Love.*

The Before Christmas

To my beloved husband … THANK YOU for all my Christmas gifts! You might ask yourself …hmmm … she hasn't opened any at the possible writing of this. So, she must have definitely snooped!! I knew I shouldn't have put her gifts under the tree early!

Well, you are wrong my love. I have never been one to snoop. Those are not the gifts I am referring to, but the ones already given.

Tears are coming as I think of the great gift you have given me to enable me to give to others so lavishly with our one income that you work so diligent and faithful at. Starting with the paper and supplies and over 100 dollars alone in postage stamps to mail our 200 Christmas cards. Then you gave gifts to the 5 families that we have been ministering to. Not only provided the money but you helped purchase as well, knowing they had very little. Then to make a trip to see my sister and supply her and her family and grandchildren with gifts…and even special ordering so I would not have to. Oh, not to forget my close friend, you gave to her and her family an abundance to help supply their needs. The gifts for the 3 young girls I mentor were over the top. We REMEMBERED the 10 stragglers…whether they were close friends, lonely singles, or family friends…we gave.

Did I mention ALL the granola, cranberry bread, cookie dough & party mix ingredients? The 20 baskets for your works were overflowing with eatable LOVE!! The church staff works so hard, it is a joy to remember them. Never can we forget our 10 wonderful neighbors all along our street.

And on Christmas weekend itself, well, you helped peel and cut LOTS potatoes for potato soup in a quart jar. Along with cobbler in a pint jar, a Christmas throw and a small Nativity…you my love made this possible. THEN you gave your Christmas day to go and deliver these Jars of Joy to 6 lonely needy households!

The numerous trips to Hobby Lobby and Wal-Mart really showed your love. You gave to every bell ringer we saw. You furnished gifts to both parents above and beyond obligatory. You out did yourself for our children. You ordered, ordered and ordered some more when I asked. You have made this such a joy. I am already filled to the brim with all you have given me this season…I am so overwhelmed with all you have allowed me to do. You supplied the finances and an extra hand when needed. Not to mention back rubs. Yes, I have already had the best Christmas! … From a JOY filled wife.

(I don't usually tell people what I'm doing – that being between me and God. Nor does He like boasting. I wrote this to Sherman and stuck it in his stocking last year, but I thought I would share a bit of my heart with you all!)

Merry Christmas

JN 2018